INTO T
THE WOMEN

By
d.j. Rangel

CONTENTS

For Dianne
With thanks for your friendship,
Your companionship on fun adventures,
And for acts of kindness and generosity
too numerous to
count

... Come my friends,
Tis not too late to seek a newer world
Push off, and setting well in order smite
The sounding furrows, for my purpose holds
To sail beyond the sunset ...

Alfred, Lord Tennyson
Ulysses (1842)

THE TEA PARTY

*Thank God for tea! What would
the world do without tea? --- how did it
exist? I am glad I was not born before
tea.*

Sidney Smith
Lady Holland's Memoir (1855)

THE TEA PARTY

I DIDN'T WANT TO GO, BUT I WENT.

Not gracefully. Not without resentment and complaining. But I didn't cry.

I cried when we left after Mama's passing. I cried for my mother, but mostly I cried for myself because I had to do all the packing. Even at fourteen, I knew that the throwing out, the giving away, the leaving behind was the hardest part. What did I know about which things were important and which were not?

So I sniveled and pouted and made clear to Papa and my older brothers that it wasn't my fault if things they later needed did not make it into the wagon. My brothers replied sharply and with disgust that I wasn't a baby anymore and if things they needed were left behind it surely would be my fault. Papa didn't say anything.

I was born in Boston but started school in Harrisburg. Mama saw to it that I had a pretty new dress for my baptism in Columbus, but I put my hair up the day I packed her things in Indianapolis. Papa looked at me as I took Mama's place beside him in the wagon, and I looked back at him with my chin up. He flicked the reins to get the horses started.

Papa waited three years in Springfield for my brothers to come home from fighting the Johnny Rebs, but they never did. This time, I knew what to take and what to give away, and what to leave on the porch for the rag collector. And I knew that the young man who handed me into Papa's wagon would not be in some distant place to hand me down from it when it came time to unload.

I nodded to that young man and waved my handkerchief as Papa released the brake and set the team into motion. The young man lifted his hand, and my best friend Leonora, standing beside him, waved her handkerchief back at me and tried to look sad. They were a handsome couple.

When I turned to face the streets leading us out of town, my back stayed straight and my eyes stayed dry. I was nineteen years old.

In Independence, I saw my first red Indian. He was missing an eye, he was dirty, and he was drunk. At least, that's what Papa said. The man leaned against a store post and as the wagon passed by he vomited into the street. The storekeeper, shouting, rushed out with a raised broom and the Indian lurched out of my sight.

In St. Joseph we joined others who talked of land and opportunity in California. Our wagon became an added knot in a string of wagons filled with people like my papa who believed troubles could be left behind. And perhaps they could.

Before we left St. Joe, I saw a trio of red Indian children. Like the man in St. Louis, the little girls were dirty, their ragged gingham dresses too short, and they were barefoot. From their vacant faces and empty stares as we passed by I presumed them stupid, but Papa said theirs were the faces of hopelessness.

Would Papa look like that, I wondered, if he couldn't leave his troubles behind? Or would he look like the Indian I saw weeks later in Lincoln who gazed at me with contempt as I stepped off the porch of the mercantile? Fierce pride radiated from this man's wide-set shoulders and belligerent stance. Like the others I'd seen, this red Indian was ragged, but even so he held his troubles close to his heart and nursed them as one would a child.

Papa said such men were dangerous.

Troubles, however, can't always be left behind. Some wait just around the next bend ready to latch onto one's hopes. "Merry hell," Papa said, gazing at our broken wheel. This particular trouble was beyond his ability to repair, as well as beyond the ability of the others. And it couldn't be abandoned.

Wives and families sat in their wagons looking nervous and frightened as the menfolk joined Papa in staring at the wheel, hoping, I suppose, for divine revelation. The men shook their heads and lifted their gaze to the surrounding hills. Weeks had gone by since we'd seen an Indian, but we'd heard plenty about them and always in warning.

Pursing his lips, Papa considered the wheel, then looked at our wagon full of my things and my mother's things. Finally, he looked at me. I shook my head. "I'm not leaving my home," I said.

After a moment, he nodded. He shook hands with the men and, when they'd rejoined their waiting families, tipped his hat to their womenfolk as the wagons lumbered past us.

We knew of no settlements ahead, but there was one five days behind that had a smithy of sorts. Papa would take the horse, dragging the wheel, while I watched over the wagon and oxen.

Before Papa left, the young man who had often ridden beside our wagon came racing back to tell of an abandoned cabin about a mile ahead. With his help, we moved part of the foodstuffs there and some of the bedding. He also helped Papa clear the chimney. Holding my hand in both of his, he told me he would look for me in California. Then he rode off.

Papa left the next morning, leaving me alone. I fed the oxen and surveyed my surroundings. A meadow fit like a woman's collar around the cabin, the small clear stream meandering through it adding a pretty ribbon. But rugged hills rose in the distance looming over a wooded expanse surrounding the meadow on all sides. They, and the dark woods, both frightened and comforted me.

The cabin's one room seemed a palace after the confines of the wagon, but it was a palace with gaps in its log walls and holes in the roof. Its entry had a sagging door hanging by one rotting leather hinge. No pane or shutters protected its single window; its floor was the earth upon which it sat. The fireplace and chimney were sound, however, and a couple of packing crates nailed to the wall served as shelves.

Someone had left behind a table. I wondered why.

The cabin needed a good cleaning, but my broom was still in the wagon.

Going to the door, I looked out again, wondering what to do with myself. Just beyond, only a few steps away, the ruts of passing wagons cut deep into the sod. My gaze tracked the line of them to the far horizon but saw no human movement or wisp of smoke from distant campfires. The light westerly breeze brought no distant laughter of children or plaintive low of a cow anxious to be milked. For the first time in my life, I was alone.

Papa's troubles … and mine, too … sat a mile away, my mother's and my grandmother's furniture protected under its white canvas. Packed in boxes were my mother's wedding dishes and the doll her own papa had given her when she was a little girl and that I had played with, too.

I thought of the Indian who had kept his troubles next to his heart.

It took me four trips and most of the day to bring my broom, the dishes, my sewing box and the mantle clock, and another three days to bring the rest. Much of what I brought I had to unpack from their boxes so I could carry it piece-meal. Once I had everything in the cabin, I arranged and rearranged and arranged again. The sight of pretty things around me, the feel and smell of them, kept loneliness at bay. When Papa returned, I would repack.

Twelve days went by before I saw him riding toward me, a shimmering figure in the distance. He'd left the wheel by the wagon, he said. I returned to it with him and helped as much as I could. We managed enough that we could hitch up the oxen, and by stopping often to adjust the wheel, got the wagon to the cabin. There we could unload the furniture and place it in the cabin while Papa fixed the wheel properly.

The bed, the bureau, the chests, my great grandmother's secretary, all had to be placed just so, I told him when we arrived at the cabin door. That was when Papa finally noticed what I had retrieved in his absence. He looked at Mama's wedding dishes sitting on one of the shelves, and looked at her teapot, centered on a cutwork cloth on the table. He gazed at the rocking chair tucked in one corner with an empty crate upturned beside it so that my sewing box was handy. He looked at me.

We sat at the table that night to have our supper. We didn't eat from tin plates but from my mother's china.

The next morning, Papa refit the wheel and drove the wagon around the meadow a couple of times to test it. When he returned, he parked it to the side of the cabin instead of at its door. "Winter's coming on," he said. "I expect there's already snow in the passes, so we'll leave in the spring." With foodstuffs now at hand, I fixed a good supper that night.

Papa repaired the cabin roof, rebuilt the corral and rigged a shelter for the animals. In the meadow, he scythed what he could for winter fodder, which bared the ruts there even more. They stood out like scars on a shorn head. I gathered as much fuel as I could find for winter fires.

The two of us re-chinked the cabin walls and I hung the extra quilts over them to further keep out drafts. At times during the long evenings that winter, I watched Papa stare at them, his gaze unfocused and distant. Did he, like me, recall a party, a Sunday meeting or autumn afternoon when those who had been a part of our lives had worn the shirts and vests, aprons and dresses their patterns were made from?

In the morning after such evenings, Papa always went to the wagon, still parked beside the cabin. He would run his hands over it, as if searching for broken bones, and check all its fastenings, much as one would the coat of a careless child. When he returned inside, stomping snow from his boots and pulling his mittens off with his teeth, I had tea cakes waiting, or a dried apple cobbler.

Winter passed at last, an exuberant spring chivying at its heels. As anxious as the springtime, Papa told me he was going into town for traveling supplies. He would take the wagon, he said, and have the smithy check it out. We would load it on his return.

I stood at the open doorway and watched the wagon follow the trail back in the direction from which we'd come last fall, watched the once winter-faded ruts spring forth bright and rejuvenated behind its wheels. In the opposite direction, headed west, they remained vague shadows. This year, I knew, Papa's wagon would be the first to trace them sharply upon the land for others to follow. Another winter would find them harder to smooth, but by then we would be in California. Perhaps.

A few days later and as I bent over a packing box, I heard a pop. It took a moment for me to realize that what I heard was a rifle shot. I stilled and heard the sound again. Pop, pop, pop. Just like that … pop pop pop. Soft, because the sound was distant, yet somehow reaching my ear distinctly, as if each pop were cut from the air through which it traveled.

I went to the door and looked out. The meadow lay golden-green and still. A lark called, and a breeze lightly shifted my skirt and rippled over the meadow's grasses. I lifted my face to a cloudless sky. At last I turned back into the cabin and continued packing. There wasn't much more of it to do. Except for items I needed to keep handy until the very last, or items we used on the trail, I was almost finished.

The day crept on. With our personal things in their boxes and Mama's furniture placed haphazardly near the door ready to be loaded in the wagon when Papa returned, the cabin held nothing to surround me with but loneliness.

But I had left one last quilt on a wall, and my grandmother's teapot sat ready to brew a last cup of tea. A cloth still covered the table we had found in the cabin, although we would leave the table behind when we left. Mama's bed was still made.

A last supper, a last night, an early hurried breakfast and we would be gone. When Papa returned.

Night came. Not a last night, after all, because he wasn't back. I prepared and ate a leisurely breakfast. Outside the cabin door, morning bloomed still and cool; across the dew-wet meadow, a lark leaped for the sky, trilling. *I'll make a brown betty*, I thought.

With the betty filling the cabin with its fragrance, I opened a box and took out Mama's dishes. I found her doll and took it out, too, placing it on the bed. Taking the quilt from the wall, I folded it neatly. I made tea.

And they were there, rushing through the open door with howls and raised weapons. I turned from the fireplace, holding the poker, the lid to the Dutch oven dangling from its end. Perhaps the man saw it as a weapon. I don't know. But he looked at it and laughed.

Behind him, another man deliberately smashed one of my mother's cups. I gasped and dropped the poker. It hit the side of the fireplace with the lid still on its end, the clang of metal reverberating in the room. A rifle stock was raised ... to brain me, I suppose ... but I had already picked up another cup and its saucer, my attention only on the man who had just broken one of Mama's dishes.

If I was going to die, it would be in a home that was a home. My trouble was here and now, and I would hold it as closely to my heart as these men did, but they must recognize and appreciate it. That was only fair.

The man would have swept it from my grasp, but I raised my hand to him and looked at him the way I often looked at my papa. Deliberately, I reached for the teapot and poured tea into the cup in my hand. Placing it on the table, I spooned sugar from the sugar bowl into it and stirred gently. When I picked up the cup and saucer again, I held them so that the flower pattern was clearly visible. I showed it to the man who was so quick to break things. He drew a hand back, but before he could swipe again, I handed the cup and saucer to him. Startled, he took them, even held them delicately, as I had.

Then I poured three more cups of tea, added sugar, and handed them round, all the while calling the men's attention to the pattern, the flowers, the scrolling leaves, the beauty of the design of my mother's cups and saucers and on her dessert plates. The men's gaze followed my tracing finger, and once I knew they had really looked at the dishes, I spooned up the apple betty. One of the men would have eaten his immediately but I raised my hand and made him wait until I had served them all.

There were not enough chairs, though they might not have sat in them anyway, but at my invitation the men sat on the floor, their legs crossed, their weapons across their laps. I sat, too, and sipped tea. I was afraid the betty would choke me. It had no such effect on the men. In two bites, they ate the betty, utensils unnecessary to their enjoyment. Since the tea was too hot to gulp, they sucked at it with a great smacking of lips. I took around the teapot again, this time pouring only dabs for the pot was almost empty. When the men were finished, each replaced his cup on its saucer as I did.

They stood, and I looked around the cabin at the things they would take and the things they would break. But before they destroyed anything, I wanted them to know about it, wanted them to know and be able to tell their wives and anyone else to whom they might give my family's things. I unfolded the quilt and traced out its pattern, pointing out the scraps of its makeup and telling the stories of where they came from. I showed them how to wind the mantle clock, explained the ingredients in making the apple betty, and showed them my grandmother's written recipe for it. They didn't understand a word I said, of course, but I could see their curiosity and their shrewdness.

At last, I had no more to tell.

They left without killing me. I don't know why. Nor did they smash anything. But they took. Each man walked out of my home with the cup and saucer he had used for tea. They didn't ask for them, either. One also took my mother's doll. But when the youngest eyed my teapot and reached, I scowled, and he pulled his hand back when another of the men scowled at him, too.

Perhaps they didn't kill me because they thought it impolite, having eaten my food. If so, they could afford the good manners. A woman alone doesn't fit into known society. Perhaps they thought I would be gone soon; other red Indians would find me, or other white men, either for marriage or for rape and murder. Or they thought I would leave my home and walk back to the nearest town and be absorbed by it, leaving the cabin behind and my things.

I thought about that last when I walked the ruts Papa had recarved when he returned to the town for supplies. I thought about it when I found his body and the overturned wagon. I thought about California. When the first of the wagons going in that direction came upon me, I was stabbing at the ground trying to bury Papa where he lay.

Instead, the men helped me get his body and the wagon back to the cabin, and they helped me bury Papa in a place he might have enjoyed, a spot not far from the ruts running in front of the cabin. One of the women gave me a rose cutting to mark the site, and another offered a cutting of lilac to plant by the cabin's front door. I'm sure they thought it wasted effort, that I would never see them bloom, but still they wanted to be kind and knew what my heart craved.

I smiled and thanked them and gave them tea using Mama's good dishes. We sat at the table, a cloth covering its scarred top, and nibbled on tea cakes with napkins covering our laps. When the women left, their hands trembled as they clasped mine in farewell. My own did not.

All that spring and summer, wagons in their hundreds passed by my home. Sometimes a train stopped for a while so the menfolk could find out what I knew of the trail ahead, but what I knew was never of any value to them. Sometimes they stopped and circled in the meadow for a night or two.

From my own experience I knew what the light in my cabin window probably meant to them.

Because of those wagons I was able to make a living of sorts, trading my cooking for supplies, re-trading supplies for other supplies or sometimes for the kinds of repairs I couldn't do myself.

If they stopped long enough, I invited the women to tea. I wrote the invitations on scraps of precious paper and the women arrived with their dresses smoothed and their hair tidied. Because of the large numbers, we sat on boxes at tables made of boxes, but cushions added softness beneath our rumps and a lace-edged cloth graced the tray beneath Mama's china, though often I was forced to supplement it with the more everyday dishes. Sipping tea, we chatted of the latest fashions and of prized bonnets packed away for more settled times. We spoke of the ladies' societies to which we'd once belonged and of the lectures we had once attended, of former neighbors and extended families we'd left behind.

After the wagons passed on, items were often left behind, sometimes by accident and sometimes on purpose. When the women left things in my cabin, however, it was not by accident but with my promise that the silver tea set, the bureau, the clock, the mirror, the books, the framed pictures, the christening gown or scrapbook would someday be sent on to them when they had an address. They left each item neatly wrapped, if possible, but always carefully identified. By late summer I had added a second room for storage.

Yet while the women envied the home I had made, I could tell they also pitied my aloneness. And the men seemingly had no understanding of a woman who would not give up her kitchen garden to go with them. I wasn't sure I understood it myself, but I knew where I belonged, and I was staying put. None of the men who took time from their travels to come sparking talked about the end of the trail. They talked only of the trail itself.

Beyond my door, the ruts deepened. Where there were two, now there were six and the beginning of eight. I felt like a sand bank in the middle of a river, the current sweeping everything before it but me. When winter dusted the ruts with snow, then wiped them out entirely, I was relieved. My cabin became an island in a calm lake of white.

The peace didn't last long. Hearing a noise outside my door one midmorning, I opened it to find a rabbit carcass on the porch stone. Standing just beyond were the three men who had come to kill me the spring before. They stood silently, wrapped in fur, each cradling a rifle in one arm, the opposite hand cradling a cup and saucer.

Slowly, I picked up the rabbit by its hind legs. The men didn't move. I backed into the cabin. They still didn't move. Heart slamming, I gestured to invite them in.

I made tea in my grandmother's teapot and when it had steeped, poured out into each cup, adding sugar generously. I noticed as I did so that every cup and saucer was whole and perfect, with not so much as a tiny chip. As before, the men sat on the floor. A Turkey rug covered it now, but I spread a cloth anyway, one I had embroidered.

We took tea. I passed around a plate of tiny cakes.

When the teapot was empty and the cakes devoured, the older man stood and began to talk. I did not understand what he said, but I knew what he was telling me. He told me about the pattern embroidered in beads on his shirt and the woman who had done the work. He pointed out the pattern on his moccasins and stooped to trace it with a finger. Indicating the feather tied to a braid dangling beside his face, he told me about that, too. When he finished, he sat, and the next man stood and spoke, and then the young man. I looked at the patterns closely, for they were quite beautiful, but I wasn't quite sure about the feathers. They were too near the men's faces for me to examine as carefully.

With their recitations over, the men rose together and gathered their furs about them. But when they would have placed their cups and saucers in the pouches they wore crossed over their shoulders, I raised a hand to stop them. Taking the dishes, I carefully washed and dried each setting before giving it back to its new owner. Better, I supposed, than having Mama's fine set in pieces with my blood spattered over it.

On an afternoon two days later, I opened my front door to find an ocean of red Indians flowing across my meadow. Many trudged beside riders, and some rode on sledges pulled behind horses. A few sledges, piled with what looked like hide-covered packages, were pulled by dogs. Other dogs ran freely, yipping and barking, with children laughing and cavorting among them. I slammed the cabin door.

When at last I gathered sufficient courage to open the window shutter and peer out, I found the area before my cabin pulsing with activity. All across the meadow, tepees were going up, the women, who seemed to be doing most of the work, erecting their homes right on top of the wagon ruts, once again exposed as the snow was trampled to slush by hundreds of feet.

We didn't bother each other, those people and I. They went about their business and I went about mine, the cold and blowing drifts keeping us close to our homes and huddled around our hearths. But spring eventually breathed down upon us.

Opening my door to let in its freshness, I found my three gentlemen callers, cups and saucers in hand, standing silently at the doorstep. We took tea, but this time there was little to say. We understood each other better now. They left, and the next day the village left as well. In a few weeks, the first wagons appeared to redefine the flattened ruts and deepen them even more.

That summer I took my own wagon to the town where my father had the wheel fixed. There I filed on the meadow and all the land around it. It was more land than I needed, and I wasn't sure I could hold it. At that time and in that place, deeds often didn't mean much, but the land was my trouble and I would hold it close to my heart for as long as I could.

Deeds certainly meant little to the people following the ruts, and I was not foolish enough to try and stop a flood whether it trespassed or not. Again, I traded with the people on the wagons so that by the end of the summer I had added a wood floor to my cabin and a porch. My lilac bloomed; at my father's graveside, so did the roses. I did not lack for callers, both gentlemen and ladies. I had to add another storeroom. As autumn approached, the river of wagons slowed to a trickle, then stopped completely, and I knew the passes were filled with snow.

The village returned, but there seemed fewer tepees this time, and the people seemed quieter. When the men came for tea, one of them had a terrible scar running the length of his arm, and the youngest's cup had a tiny chip. When I would have replaced it, he shook his head.

Snow came in howling blasts that winter, the wind lashing and whipping about the cabin and hammering at my door. It was not an easy time. Perhaps because of the harsh winter, there were fewer wagons that spring. By midsummer, what had been a river had slowed to a rill. By early autumn, the stream was dry.

I made my home snug and ready, yet only a handful came to set up their tepees in my meadow that winter, and only one man came to my cabin for tea. He sat in a chair at my table. Instead of teacakes, I prepared a stew. When spring came and the village left, I found his cup and saucer on my doorstep. I cradled them in my hands for a long time before I washed and dried the setting and placed it on the shelf; not with Mama's other dishes, but in a spot of its own.

That summer, a week could go by between the passing of the now much shorter wagon trains; eventually, the wagons passed singly, no longer links in huge chains as they'd once been. Few stopped and even fewer traded. I had enough to manage for a while but wasn't sure what I would do after that.

Fifteen people came back to my meadow that winter, the women erecting only four tepees. This time they placed them up close to my cabin, chicks nestling up to a broody hen. The women went about their work quietly, without teasing or gossiping to mark the occasion. The infrequent laugh of a child caused them to pause in their work and exchange small smiles. I counted six very young children, one of them a babe in arms, three older girls, two middle-aged women, and four men. Three of the men were old and stooped, the fourth the young man who had taken tea with me.

He no longer looked young. When he came to my door, he had two children with him, one a boy of about four, the other one of the older girls, about twelve. I filled plates ... not my mother's good ones ... with cornbread, beans, and a rare bit of venison.

That spring, the tepees did not come down.

A few wagons passed by; some stopped but most did not, their drivers staring hard at the tepees before flicking the reins to continue on. Occasionally, one of them spat. Of the wagons that stopped, none of the women took tea.

I bought cattle and managed to hold my land. My neighbors didn't like us, but they tolerated us. Our money often kept the bank open.

Over the years, I received a few letters asking me to

forward items left in my storeroom. I did so immediately. I haven't received such a letter in a long time now. Sitting in neat stacks on shelves kept free of dirt and rodents, the pieces wait to be claimed. Furniture left behind remains under dust covers and is frequently rubbed with oil. Each item is still labeled with the name of the woman who left it.

The main road has bypassed us, but the ruts before my door still shadow the meadow, though they are covered by lush grass in summer and snow in winter. On occasion, one of the grandchildren helps my husband down the porch steps and walks with him into their midst. The two plant their feet apart, throw their shoulders back, and face east. I remember the warriors who came to knock out my brains. Then slowly the man and child pivot. The ghostly undulations marking the ruts continue westward, beyond sight and knowing.

My husband spits.

Tired now, he returns to the porch, and I serve him hot sugared tea in Mama's good cup and saucer.

PREACHER MAN

Whither thou goest, I will go;
And where thou lodgest, I will lodge;
Thy people will be my people,
And thy God my God

The Book of Ruth

PREACHER MAN

I WAS WEEDING THE ROSES ALONG OUR FRONT FENCE WHEN I saw him comin'.

Our farmhouse sits at the road with the rest of the farm stretchin' behind, so I had a clear view of it, east and west. The road itself doesn't get much traffic, Sikesborough two miles to the east bein' only a small farmin' community. Heck, even Dukesville, ten miles to the west and the county seat, wasn't much bigger. Days could go by without any travelers passin' by our front gate, neither goin' or comin'. When they did, we usually knew who they were and why they were goin' or where they were comin' from.

But this was a stranger, settin' atop his mule just allowin' it to amble along, slow as molasses syrup. As he got closer, I saw he was deeply engrossed in a book, and when he was closer still, I saw that book was a Bible.

At our gate, the mule stopped, maybe because I was standin' there, my dress blowin' sideways in the light breeze, my bonnet hangin' down the back of my neck.

It took a minute or two for the rider to notice he wasn't goin' nowhere. When he did, he looked up and saw me standin' at the gate watching him, my face prob'ly showin' I was just short of laughin' outright.

He closed his Bible real slow, keepin' a finger in it to mark his place. And then he smiled.

With a long strong-boned face and heavy brows, he wasn't a handsome man. But when his mouth curved into a smile, his eyes smiled with it.

He sat atop his mule and just looked at me with his smilin' eyes for a long minute, and I looked at him and smiled back. My hands gripped two pickets on the gate and his mule snuffled at the fence protecting the roses. In the distance a hen cackled.

"I'm Henry Clayton McElroy," he finally said, and his voice was as soft and mellow as good Kentucky whiskey.

"I'm Idabel Joiner Kensey," I replied.

"Idabel," he repeated, the one word wrapping around me as thick and warm and comfortable as a wool cloak on a cold day. And he nodded as if agreein' to something.

My knees went to water.

"Idabel Joiner Kensey," he said then, his voice now strong and sure, "I'm goin' to marry you."

Now I'm not much to look at, bein' short and stubby with carroty hair and the freckles to go with it. Still, I'd had my share of courtin'. The boys in rural Tennessee don't have that many to choose from. The girls don't have that many, neither.

"All right," I said, and it was my turn to nod. "Would you care to stay to supper?"

"I've a callin' down the road," he replied as if he wished it wasn't so, but he sat straighter and brought the mule to attention. "I'll be back in a couple of days and will stay to supper then. Have your bag packed and be ready, for we've places to go." He shifted his Bible to his other hand so he could tip his hat.

"You a preacher man?" I asked as he turned the mule to head once more in the way he'd been goin'.

That smile again. "I am. You're a little thing. Do you think you can handle it?"

"I do."

"I like your choice of words," he replied with a chuckle. A flick of his heels and he set the mule to movin', a little faster this time and with more purpose.

I took it he was anxious to get done with what he had to do so he could come back.

It wasn't a couple of days. It was a full week, but I packed my bags and stood firm against my brothers' and sister's teasin' and my parents' worries.

And sure enough, when I looked out our front window one afternoon, I saw him arrive at our front gate. He was riding his mule and was leadin' another.

I hurried out to our front porch to welcome him, but he stayed atop his mule and just looked at me like I was somethin' good to look at.

"You still comin' with me, Idabel Joiner?" he asked.

"I am, Mr. McElroy. But first, supper's ready and my daddy's waitin'.

"Of course," he said formally, and swung down from the mule.

When he stood on the porch beside me, I saw just how tall and gangly he was, his knobby wrists pokin' out of his shirtsleeves as if the garment was too small. But he was still a fine figure of a man, if I do say so.

My daddy had his reservations. I could see them written all over his face even if he never voiced them. Mama looked only at me as I stood proudly beside Mr. McElroy, the top of my head not quite reachin' his shoulder. "You sure?" she asked.

"I am," I replied.

"Best set the table then. There'll be nine of us tonight."

My easy-goin' daddy still could find no smile, but he and Mr. McElroy and the boys washed up on the back porch while we females got the table set, Mama decidin' to use her company tablecloth and dishes.

We all set down and Daddy gave Mr. McElroy a long look. "I'll leave it to you to ask the blessin', Preacher," he said. It wasn't a request.

As if it was the greatest gift Daddy could have given him, Mr. McElroy replied, "I would be honored," and he held his hands out on either side. It took us a second to realize this would not be the usual foldin' your hands in your lap kind of prayer.

We all joined hands.

"Lord," Mr. McElroy began, his eyes closed, his face serene, but with no doubt he was commanding God's attention. His voice reached out, encircled our kitchen table and seemed to float right through the ceiling and straight up to Heaven. I imagine the angels stopped their singin' just so they could listen. Certainly we listened, and God's grace comin' through Mr. McElroy's voice surely surrounded us like the golden mantle it's been called.

At the amen, comin' soon enough that the fried chicken and mashed potatoes didn't get cold, nobody said a word for a second, not even my little brother who usually used 'amen' as a signal to make a lightning reach for the nearest serving bowl.

Mama's soft sigh broke the stillness. Daddy nodded. "Thank you, Preacher," he said, and this time I heard acceptance.

That night, Mama and Daddy offered Mr. McElroy the boys' bed, sayin' the boys would sleep in the barn, but Mr. McElroy declined, sayin' he was used to sleepin' in barns, let the boys keep their bed. Mama and Daddy looked at each other, Mama frowning a bit.

Mama went to gather blankets for him to use and Daddy found a lantern. Daddy walked with Mr. McElroy to the barn and I guess helped him get situated. As usual, I slept with my sisters at what would be my last night in my parents' house.

Right after breakfast the next morning, the boys and Daddy headed out to their morning chores. For the last time, I helped Mama wash up the breakfast dishes. With the kitchen in order and feelin' a little weepy, I took off my apron and headed out the back door. It was time to go.

But on the porch, I found Mr. McElroy eyin' the boxes and cartons I planned to take with us. And for the first time, he looked at me with uncertainty in his eyes.

"Idabel," and I heard the pain in his voice, "we only have the mules."

Just then, Daddy and my oldest brother came around the barn. They were ridin' in our old buckboard and Mr. McElroy's two mules were pullin' it.

Mr. McElroy seemed to straighten, and he went real still.

Daddy jumped down and came up to the porch. "Preacher," he said, "Idabel has things her ma wants to give her and its more than your mules can carry. Call this ol' wagon a weddin' present. She's old, but she's reliable." Daddy's smile was all amiability.

I may have stood not quite to his shoulder, but I could feel the stubborn pride fairly radiatin' off Mr. McElroy at that moment. I took his hand, ready to leave everything behind if need be.

"I thank you kindly," Mr. McElroy said stiffly, "but the Lord will provide for our needs. He always has so far, and I know Idabel and I will find ways to manage."

"The Lord *has* provided," Daddy said, and there was nothing amiable about him at all.

I stood silent, but I pressed Mr. McElroy's hand.

And suddenly Mr. McElroy smiled that smile that included his eyes. "So He has, and I thank you for bein' his instrument." There was a smile in his whiskey voice, too. He shook Daddy's hand.

Daddy was quick to unbend. "Glad to do it," he replied. "Idabel's a good girl and a treasure. You're headed west, you say?"

Mr. McElroy reached down and picked up a box like it weighed nothin' at all. It had taken both my sisters and me to get it to the porch. "I'm called," he answered, placing the box carefully in the wagon.

"Dukesville's ten miles west of here," Daddy said. "It's the county seat. They have a justice of the peace. There's also a Baptist church, a Methodist church, and a Catholic church."

"It is my intention to take advantage of the fact," Mr. McElroy said.

Mr. McElroy was acquainted with the Dukesville Baptist preacher and that evening we spent the night as man and wife in a real hotel. It was the last solid roof I would have over my head for several months.

*

"Where in the west is your calling?" I asked Mr. McElroy one evening as we were eating our burned supper around a campfire. Even after several weeks I still hadn't learned the knack of campfire cooking and I was gettin' anxious for a real stove. But burned or not, we ate what we had. The foodstuffs Mama and Daddy had sent with us were getting down to almost nothin'.

"I reckon I'll know when I get there," my husband said around a mouthful of burned pone.

"You lookin' for a church?"

"I'm lookin' for the place to build one," he replied. "In the meantime, this great earth is our church. It's beautiful, ain't it?"

I looked up at the star-filled sky above us. "It is," I agreed. But out of the range of the fire, I felt the breath of chill air that hinted at the coming autumn.

Mr. McElroy was in no hurry to get wherever it was he was goin'. Our wagon was always pointed west, but his call to preach seemed to descend upon us whenever two or three was gathered together, as the sayin' goes.

It wouldn't stay two or three for long. That dark whiskey voice of his would ring out, wrapping the benevolence of God's love around all who heard it, and before you knew it the two or three had become twenty or fifty or a hundred out on some open prairie near a town. Lo an' behold, we had us a revival meetin'. Which was fine by me. While Mr. McElroy was preachin' I made sure a collection plate got passed.

Our mules had to be fed and cared for if they were goin' to carry us on down the road west, I told Mr. McElroy the first time I did it and he exclaimed, not at all pleased. Truthfully, there wasn't much on the plate. Farmin' folk don't have much cash money to spare, but we had next to none at all.

"The Lord will provide for us, Idabel," Mr. McElroy scolded gently.

"Oh, He has," I told him. "Think of the loaves and fishes, Mr. McElroy. Just like in that story, everyone at the meetin' brought a little somethin' and the Lord made it enough for all to eat their fill and even provided leftovers." On the last day of the meetin' those leftovers usually found their way to our wagon, but I didn't remind him of that. "Loaves and fishes won't help the mules do God's work, however, Mr. McElroy, so He provides for them in a different way. These few coins will provide Lucy and Lucifer with new shoes so they can carry us west."

Frowning, Mr. McElroy looked at those nickels and pennies for a long moment, then he looked a Lucy and Lucifer placidly chomping the tough grass near the wagon. He looked west. Last of all, he looked at me. His eyes smiled.

"The Lord has provided," he agreed. But he scrupulously pulled out ten percent and put it in the collection plate of the first church we came to before we left the area.

And so we continued west.

By and by, however, nature took its course. I was expecting and without a single woman to tell me about the ins and outs of the thing. I didn't know nothin' 'bout birthin' a baby. Why, I was thirteen before I found out they didn't come in the midwife's big black purse. Now I was rememberin' Mama's moans of pain and my daddy lookin' scared and walkin' the floor in front of the bedroom door before my youngest brother was born.

"Do you know how to birth a baby?" I asked Mr. McElroy when he lifted his head from his perusal of the Bible text. I was drivin' the mules as I always did when he was readin', otherwise no tellin' where we would wind up.

"I do not." He patted my knee. "But the Lord will provide, Idabel. The Lord will provide like he always does." And my husband went back to his readin'.

I hoped he knew what he was talkin' about. Unlike Mr. McElroy, I didn't put my whole faith in the Lord. I put my faith in the faith of Mr. McElroy.

In a few days, however, we came to a town large enough to have a doctor and while Mr. McElroy paid a visit to the reverend of the white church on down the street, I paid a visit to the doctor. I asked lots of questions; he gave me lots of answers. He didn't seem happy that there was only me and Mr. McElroy and a mule-pulled wagon, but that's the way it was and the way it was goin' to be. When Mr. McElroy came to fetch me, the doctor pulled him aside and gave him a few answers, too. As Mr. McElroy helped me back into the wagon, he looked pale and troubled.

He did most of the drivin' after that and often stopped early so we could camp near a town or a farmhouse. Sometimes the farmer's wife would invite us in to spend the night on a real bed. When traveling with Mr. McElroy, a body learns a lot about the kindness of strangers.

So it was that my faith in Mr. McElroy paid off and his faith in the Lord was justified because little Clarence Clayton McElroy was born right in the middle of a meetin' near a small town somewhere near or in Oklahoma Territory. I wasn't at the meetin', of course. I'd headed in that direction but didn't get very far. Some ladies saw my distress and took me back to the wagon and there, surrounded by women who knew what they were doin' because I sure didn't, I gave birth. Everything that doctor had told me flew right out of my head about midway through the process.

Mr. McElroy had no idea things were happenin'. In the distance I could hear his voice rollin' across the fields, but even though the sound of it was muted, the strong sure goodness of it reached out to comfort me in my travail – when I wasn't cussin' him for putting me through this in the first place, that was. Still, it was all worth it when I saw the pure loving joy in his face as he held his first born.

*

Ever westward. Sometimes we spent a week or a month or more in a community if it was needin' a fill-in for an absent preacher, though Mr. McElroy always made it clear we weren't stayin'. And sometimes the weather or the callin' had us driftin' a little more northerly or southerly. Even so, the west pulled hardest.

At some point we dipped down into Texas to make our slow way across its vastness. The settlements were few and far between now, but the Lord still hadn't called on Mr. McElroy to stop. I was beginnin' to wonder if He ever would.

Our second son was born in an Indian teepee when little Clarence was not quite three. Again, I was surrounded by women who knew what they were about. I knew a little more now, too. Mr. McElroy wasn't with me durin' the birthin'. When I asked for him, I was given to understand that birthin' was women's work and no men were allowed.

But when Charles Kensey McElroy's newborn cries rang out, I heard my husband's also, his strong joyful prayer wafting through the village bringing all other noises to a standstill as it enfolded one and all in the happiness it carried, though I doubt not one in ten of the Indians there understood a word. At the amen, the women surrounding my pallet sighed, and one of them patted my arm and said something to me with a soft smile.

We moved on, the setting sun always casting shadows behind us, until I, too, had a callin' when we lost little Clarence. He'd gone to explore down a dry creek when a flash flood hurtled from nowhere, carryin' him away. It took us three days to find his small mangled body.

There was nothin' to make him a coffin out of, so I wrapped him in my great grandmother's quilt that Mama had sent with me so long ago and laid my child in the pitifully shallow grave that Mr. McElroy scraped out of the rocky desert soil. Through his own tears, Mr. McElroy also fashioned a wobbly cross out of two branches from a stunted mesquite tree.

As he gave up our little Clarence to the Lord, Mr. McElroy's voice held no music, nor did it ring out over that barren land. He held my hand with one of his and in his other he held his Bible up close to his heart. I wondered which he took most comfort from, if any. In my other hand, I held

Charles' small fingers. Mr. McElroy's amen was a choked sob.

"Mr. McElroy," I said as we climbed back into the wagon, just the three of us now but I carried the beginnings of another in my belly. "Mr. McElroy, in the next settlement we will make our home."

He sat still with the reins in his hand and looked west toward a sky painted with all God's gorgeous colors, but I don't think he saw them. His shoulders slumped and he looked like an old man. Then he nodded and gave the mules the signal to head out. "All right," he said.

*

Turned out, the next settlement was three sorrowful days down the road. The only one given to chatter through those three days was little Charles.

Suggens Crossing was just that, the intersection of two trails, one goin' north-south, one goin' east-west. It had three saloons, a mercantile, a livery stable and smithy, a bank, and a combined bath house-barbershop. There were a few houses. There was no school and there was no church. There was a cemetery, however, such as it was.

We asked around and learned there was an abandoned cabin on the edge of town. Nobody seemed to own it, and nobody objected when we moved into it. One room was all it had, but the roof was good.

When folks learned that Mr. McElroy was a preacher they asked if he would do a little preachin' for them. Truth to tell, it was a few of the women who asked, but they assured us they'd clean out one of the saloons for the occasion.

The whole town showed up that Sunday. You could still smell the alcohol, but the picture above the bar was covered up. The piano player knew more than the bawdy tunes he usually played, and everyone sang the old hymns with gusto. I passed the collection plate, but as I did, I couldn't help but feel Mr. McElroy's sermon wasn't all it usually was. Somehow the glad tidings didn't ring out to the heavens and roll over the crowd as they usually did. But we had just lost our oldest child and the weight of that loss was still upon us.

Once we were settled in the cabin, Mr. McElroy took the wagon and went back and retrieved Clarence's small broken body. We buried it in the Suggens Crossing cemetery. This time he would have a proper marker bearin' his name, tellin' the world whose child he was, and when he'd been born and when he died.

The Sunday meetin's in the saloon continued as the town began to realize it had been missin' something. With the women's urgin', it was agreed that a church would be built if Mr. McElroy would consent to preach in it, which he did. The community came together for the raisin', and when it was up, Mr. McElroy's prayer rang out over the saloons and the houses and the new place of worship. The sun seemed to shine all the brighter. Charles clapped his little hands and laughed. I laughed with him.

But, still, I don't think the angels stopped their singin' this time.

Our daughter, Matilda June McElroy, was born that summer. It was not an easy birth and she would be the last of our children.

Mr. McElroy continued to preach in the little church that now served as a schoolhouse during the week. Whatever came in the collection plate was his salary and I added to it by makin' pies for the new restaurant that opened up in town. By practicin' strict economy we managed to add another two rooms and a porch onto our cabin. I put a flower garden around the porch and had a vegetable garden out back.

But Mr. McElroy's sermons never regained what they used to be. I couldn't put my finger on what was missin' but I knew something was. Over time, he became quieter at home, too. Not playin' with the children as much. Not teasin' me as often.

Mattie was six months past her second birthday when an itinerant preacher came to town, showin' up just like we had almost three years ago. The town had grown over that time and could use a second church, maybe of a specific denomination this time. Mr. McElroy greeted him heartily.

But a second church wasn't to be, not then anyway.

One night, as he and I sat at the table after supper for our evenin' cup of coffee, Mr. McElroy cleared his throat. "Idabel," he said, playing with the handle of his cup, "the callin' is strong. Will you come with me?"

I was not surprised. Suggens Crossing had been my callin', not his.

His eyes smiled at me, but his mouth didn't.

"This is your home, Mr. McElroy," I said, after takin' my time and givin' his question some thought. "And I am your wife. Follow your callin', but when you feel the need for us, come home and we will welcome you gladly."

"But how will you manage without me, Idabel? The collection plate will belong to the new preacher."

I laughed. "You needn't worry about us. The Lord will provide," I reminded him, "just as He always does." That night Mr. McElroy held me close, but I made sure he was deep asleep before I shed my tears.

That September, Charles started school. I continued to make my pies but also sold to the mercantile the jams and preserves I put up. We got by. And when Ed Watson and his wife who owned the restaurant asked me if I would like to go in with them as a cook and partner, I agreed.

Mr. McElroy usually made it home about twice a year and when he did, Jim Taylor, the preacher, stepped aside and asked him to take the pulpit. At those times, Mr. McElroy was a joy to hear, his whiskey voice rolling over the congregation that packed the small church for the occasion and on up to Heaven to awaken the angels. His love rang through the dusty streets of Suggens Crossing encompasin' all who heard it.

Each time he came home, Mr. McElroy stayed a few weeks, playin' with the children, teasin' me just like he always had, and then he would head west again, leavin' the town to return to its wildish self until the next time he came home to remind them that God's eye was not only on the sparrow.

The years went by. The town grew. The railroad came through. Charles married and eventually opened a second hotel. Mattie had several beaus and couldn't decide between them. Like the town itself, they loved it when their daddy came home to bring joy and sparkle to their lives. He was home and performed the ceremony when Mattie finally made her choice.

Our family had grown by three grandchildren when he came home for the last time, arrivin' by train. After Charles and Mattie took their families to their own homes followin' our glad reunion, he sat on the sofa with me and held my hand. "I made it all the way to the Pacific Ocean," he told me, "and considered takin' a ship across it. But you know what, Idabel? I was just too tired. Also, the roar of those ocean waves was such they drowned out the callin', if there was one. I think I've done what I was supposed to do. Now I'm ready to stay put and watch the seasons pass."

"Are you wantin' to pastor another church somewhere?" I asked. "There's still a lot of empty country out there. I can go with you now. Charles and Mattie will take care of Clarence's grave."

"No," he said. "No, I think my callin's done been answered."

He looked and sounded so tired that I believed him.

That year we often sat on the porch in our rockin' chairs, holdin' hands and watchin' the world go by. Sometimes we'd laugh about the preacher man who, on first sight, told a stubby red-haired gal he was goin' to marry her. And did.

Mr. McElroy gave one last sermon inside the little church and it was a glorious thing. The town still talks about it.

He's buried beside little Clarence and I'll be joinin' him there. Soon, I think.

If you're wonderin', you won't find Suggens Crossing on a map anymore. Now the town's called McElroy. Things like that can happen when your son's the mayor.

ENOUGH

The earth, that is sufficient,
I do not want the constellations any nearer,
I know they are well where they are,
I know they suffice for those who belong to them.

Walt Whitman

Song of the Open Road

ENOUGH

JIM LAY AT HER FEET, HIS BODY CROSSHATCHED IN GORE. Where Margaret felt bewildered surprise, his dead face held only acceptance.

They had come from nowhere, from everywhere, with paint on their faces and screams in their throats; as they had come before; not often, but enough that she and Jim lived warily. Healthy fear and a fine gun had kept them alive, but insidious complacency and then the Apaches crept in, catching them unprepared.

Now Margaret placed a foot on either side of Jim's body and picked up his gun. A child clung to her skirts; another lay in the dust beside his father.

The Apaches surrounded her, screams silent as smiles curved their mouths; taunting smiles, smiles matching the hate in their eyes. Victory smiles.

She saw they were not after all in their hundreds. There were only five, the youngest perhaps fourteen, the oldest possibly in his fifties. Pulling herself up into straight-shouldered defiance, anchored by the child's grip on her skirts, her bewilderment at last gave way to sustaining anger.

Battle is an Apache's lifeblood, the heart of his campfire stories, and the men about her tensed in eager anticipation. With this woman and in this ranch-yard their prowess could be easily proven. They could not lose.

Holding the gun with both hands, Margaret looked at them in turn, meeting each pair of eyes. Then, with all her strength, she hurled the weapon to the ground so that its polished stock shattered against one of the stones lining her flower garden.

"Enough!" she said. Having been a schoolteacher before her marriage, she spoke the word with authority and in a tone that would be obeyed. But Apaches are not children to obey white schoolteachers, yet they checked their angry forward movement at witnessing the loss of a fine weapon. She had spoken their language.

"There will be no more," her voice rising like a preacher's delivering Holy Writ.

A hot wind blew her skirts against Jim's body, bloodying its hem.

She turned, not to the man wearing a bright red bandanna and whose body was masculine perfection, or to the one whose thin legs stuck out below a little round belly, but to the warrior who looked to be in his late thirties, who had a new scar running across his cheek and continuing down over his chest. The one who looked like a coyote.

"Why do you kill my family?" she demanded.

"You are Apache?"

"I am Metcalf. My mother is Mexican and my father German. My husband taught me your language when I was a child."

"Ah. Your man is Apache." As one, the five stepped forward to peer into her husband's dead accepting face.

Margaret did not move. "My husband is ... *was* ..." Her voice spiraled before she gathered it back … "Jim Metcalf. His mother was Apache, his father American. We are not Apache. We are not American or Mexican or German. Why do you kill my family?"

"You take Apache land."

"We did not take the land. Has it gone anywhere?"

"You build fences," the man said, and the others nodded in agreement.

"Fences keep the cattle in and the horses, but not the stream. Fences do not keep out the deer or the lions or the vultures. They do not keep out the Apache." She looked meaningfully at the men around her.

"Why do you sometimes kill my cows?" she asked suddenly.

The man grunted. "We are hungry, and your cows are eating our grass. Why should we not?"

"Why should my cows not eat your grass if you are eating my cows?"

The others laughed at her slyness, but the warrior merely smiled his coyote smile. "Where one comes, thousands follow, gobbling whatever is in their path," he replied. "Whites are greedy."

"But I am only one and my path stops here." Margaret's gaze dropped to the still forms of her husband and her fallen child. She reached to take the toddler's grip from her skirt and fold the small hand into her own before lifting her head once more.

"I have not gobbled, I have only fenced. With this piece of land, I have enough and need no more. And I am not white." To prove it, she thrust forward a deeply tanned fist with freckles across the back of it and a broken blister on the thumb.

The leader grunted again.

When they left, they took the horses, an iron skillet, a

package of needles, two of Jim's shirts, and her calico sunbonnet patterned with red flowers.

She buried Jim, and as best she could doctored her son Leander, for he was not dead. Ever after he had a stiff shoulder that hurt when it rained. Both boys grew tall and strong, but where Leander laughed too often, James Lee laughed seldom or not at all.

The Apaches came back many times, racing their horses around the cabin when the occupants least expected it, filling the air with their taunting screams, always leaving fear behind and the reminder of how tenuous was this partnership. They butchered a cow now and then, sometimes for meat, sometimes just to show they could. The spring, not half a mile from the cabin and the origin of the stream meandering through this corner of the desert and turning it to grassland, became a frequent stopping place.

Then they didn't come as often. And after a while, Margaret deliberately staked one of her cows under the tall cottonwood near the spring and left a blanket or two and baskets of winter corn. Nor did she look beyond the fences she and Jim had strung when finally the cow and blankets and corn remained untouched.

Soon other fences joined hers and a road ran past the far gate. When James Lee went deer hunting one day, a rancher brought him home and gave them all to understand that his fences were built to keep cows in and people out. Margaret, standing in the ranch yard with a sullen James Lee beside her, nodded silently.

She knew then that she'd better have a piece of paper defining and legalizing what her fences enclosed. She hired a lawyer and did what she ought at the courthouse. But before she put the paper away in her mother's cut glass sugar bowl on the mantle, she went to the reservation.

It took a long time, but she eventually learned that the

warrior with the coyote smile had been taken to a Florida prison. After much searching and false leads, she located the teenager. He now had only one arm and was a teenager no longer but had become leader of the ragged band of humanity Margaret saw around her. His face bore only acceptance, reminding her of Jim's, but Jim's dead face had also held peace. He smiled as he x-ed her paper, a cynical smile. "It's not much," he said, "but I suppose it has to be enough."

Leander didn't like raising cattle or keeping a garden and eventually took a storekeeping job in town. Yet even his ready laughter couldn't make him or the townspeople forget his father's mother was Apache.

"You are not Apache," Margaret reminded him again and again, "or American. You are Metcalf." But he didn't believe her.

He left the area and Margaret heard he went to California. Then she didn't know if he lived or died, for he never wrote or got in touch.

After three dry years in a row, the rancher whose fences adjoined hers, the one who hadn't liked James Lee hunting on his land, came to see her.

"My cattle are dying of thirst," he said. "Your spring is the only water source in the area still running and the stream now goes underground not a mile into my land."

He remained on his horse, mounted cowhands with drooping mustaches at either side of him. Still, under her stare, he squirmed a bit so that his saddle creaked.

"I'm sorry to hear about your cattle," she said after a long moment of looking up at him. "Come in and we'll talk about it. I'll make a pot of coffee."

They hitched their horses and went inside, each man removing his hat. Over coffee they talked of the drought, the railroad, the changing times. They did not talk of Leander, or of James Lee, or of the government. When they finished their coffee and the pie she'd also brought out, the men and Margaret walked to the spring to gaze on it as if it were an icon and they true believers.

"You may use the water," Margaret told them. "I have enough. But if your cattle are too many or you take more than your share, then both of us will see our cattle die and ourselves as well."

It struck the rancher then that neither he nor his men had seen James Lee. When he turned and found the boy, now a young man, holding a rifle and standing comfortably behind him as if he'd been there a long while, a shiver ran down his spine.

The rancher sold most of his cattle, as did Margaret, and with what was left they shared the stream. When the rains came the following year, the rancher invited James Lee to go deer hunting with him in the mountains. James Lee refused.

One morning Margaret went out to feed the chickens and found a strange horse in the corral. She eyed it silently for a long moment, then turned in a slow circle, studying the land. In the direction of the spring, smoke poked a palsied finger at the dawn sky.

The warrior no longer had the coyote look in his eye nor wore his coyote smile. As he sat in front of the wickiup beneath the cottonwood, he wore no smile at all, but he still had the terrible scar across his face and chest. "We should have allowed you to fence more," he said in his own language.

Margaret sat down in front of him. "More would have been too much," she replied.

"To an Apache, there's not enough room here to spit." His tone held disdain.

"To a Metcalf, there's enough room here to die."

They sat quietly as the sun rose to burn off the morning chill. His name was Javier and his wife, who he did not name, made coffee, serving some to Margaret in a tin cup. His green-eyed daughter stirred cornmeal into boiling water. Margaret drank her coffee and left.

Javier and his family stayed two months. Some days he helped James Lee work cattle, some days he sat in front of his wickiup and smoked. He brought Margaret a haunch of venison late one afternoon, casually dropping the bloody meat on the stepping-stone at her door. She didn't ask where he'd hunted, and the rancher never came. As unexpectedly as they'd arrived, Javier and his family left, leaving no trace of their camp near the spring except for a charred fire circle.

After that, they came two or three times a year, arriving and leaving at Javier's whim. One time when they left, his green-eyed daughter stayed behind, and James Lee built a second cabin.

Maria Elena was a quiet girl, not pretty, a little taller than most Apache women. But her eyes were not quiet and could dance with green flame and that was enough for James Lee. She put up with his erratic temper and bore him five children. Three lived past infancy.

She worked at his side through grass fires and tick fever and worked alone while Margaret kept the children and did housework for both of them over the six weeks it took James Lee to recover from a broken leg. During the years he made the bottle his master, she and Margaret again kept the ranch going.

The sheriff came in a wagon one night, with James Lee lying in the back of it, beaten to a bloody pulp by a cowboy in town drunker than he was and a better fighter with it. The trips to town stopped and the drinking. James Lee began to laugh more, as if something in his drinking years or in the fight that almost killed him had joggled loose his sense of humor.

After the sinking of the *Maine*, he talked of soldiering so he could send extra money home. He and Margaret stood in the ranch yard near the spot where his father's blood had soaked into the ground.

Margaret gazed off into the distance, the sun picking out the mousy gray in her hair and turning it to silver. "I've never met a Spaniard," she said at last, "and you are not American. You are Metcalf." She turned and went inside. James Lee then talked it over with Maria Elena. He did not go to war.

His oldest son went to France, in spite of the fact he was Metcalf and had never met a German. He never saw the shell that killed him, nor the cannon that fired it, nor met a German. His dead face, unseen by any of his family, wore a look of astonishment.

Javier came back to the ranch one last time and was buried near Maria Elena's stillborn daughter. The flowers Margaret placed upon his grave, in full knowledge that he'd not appreciate them, withered quickly. No clouds blotted the sun, and the sky shone a pale blue through the thin layer of something from a factory two hundred miles to the north, but later that afternoon a desert storm washed Margaret's flowers away. Standing inside the cabin doorway and watching the rain come down in torrents, Margaret smiled.

The land within their fences, once considered prime, took on a shabby look compared to the surrounding holdings. Other ranchers sank deep artesian wells and enlarged stock tanks, plowed the desert soil and used fertilizers to make it bloom a lush blue-green.

Margaret did no plowing except in her vegetable garden, and her fertilizer, manure and plant leavings, did not come from the feed store in town. She sank no wells, having enough water from the spring. Her cattle ate the same course brown grass they always had. Whenever the grass started to look worn out, she moved her cows or sold them.

But the water from the spring took on an under-taste, so

that one morning Margaret threw out a whole pot of coffee in disgust. Troubled, she walked out into the ranch yard and turned in a slow circle, scanning the horizon. An old woman now and her eyesight not what it used to be, she saw nothing.

A month later she sat down in the chair near the fireplace and refused to get up except to move to her bed. Maria Elena prepared her meals and washed her clothes. One of the grandsons chopped her wood and fed the chickens.

James Lee didn't tell her the spring was slowing to a trickle. In desperation and without Margaret's knowledge, he dug wells as had the other ranchers. But in spite of the occasional rains that once were enough, the land had run dry.

He sold the cattle.

As the spring and his mother died, James Lee kept vigil. Margaret went first. A week later the spring turned to mud; within another week it was dust. He never knew which neighbor's well had tapped its source. After packing or selling everything movable, he took his family and moved on.

The huge cottonwood, having shaded the spring for over a century, withered. Bare spots spread as creosote bush moved in, nature spacing the plants as regularly as if they'd been planted. A gully formed where the stream once was, its ragged ditch carrying water only in times of flood. Most of the time, the land just baked.

Eventually, the rancher from the adjoining property, the one who'd once shared the stream, came and surveyed the deserted homestead. The barns and outbuildings were already disintegrating, the main cabin would probably last another generation. A shutter, three inches thick, banged with the monotony of cannon fire against its side. He fastened it.

Pulling his hat to his brows, he shook his head, disgusted

that the Metcalfs had made no improvements to the land but allowed nature, which didn't give a damn about cattle or crops, to have its way. Now the acreage lay dead and barren. Abandoned.

When he studied the courthouse records, however, the rancher shook his head again and decided the land wasn't worth the legal tangle. Anyway, with no one on the place, he could use whatever of it was fit to use whenever he wanted.

Over the years, hunters occupied the cabins, and vandals. What fence posts didn't rot went to feed campfires, their barbed wire long since rusted away or confiscated by collectors. One whole side of Margaret's house now panels the family room of an upscale home in Phoenix to give it 'rustic charm' according to the interior decorator who suggested it.

But the weed-gutted remnants of its foundation remain, and the pile of rocks that once formed the chimney. A corner of the squared-off doorstep pokes out of the earth. The gravesites have disappeared, along with the dead cottonwood. Nothing gives indication a spring ever existed.

Stretching along highway 240, the property's back reaches are often used as a firing range. Targets are the cans and bottles left from clandestine teenage beer parties. The land is still deeded to the Metcalfs and the Apache nation, but neither have bothered to claim it.

THE PRETTIEST GIRL IN PARSON GULCH

She walks in beauty, like the night
Of cloudless climes and starry skies;
And all that's best of dark and bright
Meet in her aspect and her eyes ...

George Noel Gordon, Lord Byron
She Walks in Beauty, Hebrew Melodies (1815)

THE PRETTIEST GIRL IN
PARSONS GULCH

IT WAS NEVER GOING TO HAPPEN.

Not with the Watley nose.

She would be an old maid; or, considering Papa's wealth, more likely one of Savannah's 'maiden ladies.'

Always a maiden. A maiden till she died. She was already an aunt. She would always be an aunt. An indulgent *maiden* aunt, spoiling her nieces and nephews because she would have no children of her own to fuss over.

She would naturally be the one in the family to take care of Mama and Papa as they aged. And when they were gone, she would probably wither away, too, in a waft of rose water and lavender sachets, Mama's cameo – because Mama would probably leave it to her – pinned at the high-necked stand-up collar of her gray dress. Yes, the dress would be gray, as she herself would be gray, and it would have long tight sleeves to hide the drooping crepe-y skin of her aged arms and be high necked to show off the cameo and hide her aged crepe-y throat.

All because of the Watley nose.

Cora turned away from the dresser mirror to stare at her full-length self in the cheval mirror beside it.

Her figure wasn't bad. She pushed out nicely in front, and just as nicely in back, even without the small bustle she usually wore. Her hair, thick and abundant, she kept dressed in the latest style. It was a rich brown, like Papa's.

And she was taller than most. Like Papa. With snapping brown eyes. Like Papa's.

And she had the Watley nose. Exactly like Papa's.

Papa, and her brothers who looked like him, including the dominating Watley nose, were all handsome men. She, on the other hand, who also looked like him, was plain as a fence post.

Her three sisters looked like her mother. Average height, dainty figures, and with noses that fit their faces. And all married. Two of them, younger than she, had children.

Cora sat down on the side of her bed and stared at her dancing slippers. Sticking out her legs, she pointed her toes toward each other; pointed them away. Together. Away. Together. Away.

Finally, with a sigh, she lay back on the bed, her legs still dangling, and stared at the ceiling.

She'd realized at the ball tonight that her fate was well and truly sealed. Oh, she'd not been a total wallflower. She'd danced with Papa. Her brothers did their duty, as well, as had a couple of their friends. Even her brothers-in-law and a couple of Papa's friends led her onto the floor. She was a good dancer, and a good sport ... and didn't she just love *that* phrase. A few of her friends' brothers and/or husbands danced with her, too.

So, no, she had not sat alone and lonely as the dancers took to the floor. But neither had anyone danced with her who had not felt under obligation, either.

She was twenty-eight years old.

Cora set up a light staccato with her heels against the metal mattress railing and sighed again.

After a soft knock on her door, her mother entered. "I saw your light still on," she said. "Are you all right, dear?"

"I'm fine, Mama," Cora replied, not sitting up and continuing her examination of the ceiling.

Her mother sat down next to her on the side of the bed. "Did you not enjoy the evening?" she asked quietly.

Cora kept her prone position. "It was fine." A tear slipped out and ran down the side of her face and into her hair.

Mama didn't speak for a long moment, but when at last she did, she changed the subject completely. "I received a letter from your Aunt Lucille today."

"Did you?" Not really in the mood for idle conversation, Cora closed her eyes.

"She's inviting you to come visit for a while. There are few women in Parsons Gulch and she's lonely, she says."

"Aunt Lucille is married," Cora replied, still with her eyes closed. "Why should *she* be lonely?"

"A woman needs women friends sometimes," Mama replied. "Someone who understands about some things the way a man never can. With so many men and so few women, Lucille misses having another woman to talk to."

Cora slowly sat up, it finally dawning on her what her mother was saying without saying it. "Not many women?"

"Well, Lucille says there is the wife of the man who runs the general store, but she's sixty if she's a day, and there are a couple of Chinese laundresses, but they don't speak English and keep to themselves. Lucille's letter sounded as if she's terribly lonely with so many men around and so few women."

"You would allow me to travel so far away?"

"Only if it makes you happy, darling. I would keep you with me forever, you know that. This is your home, and I love you. But sometimes a young handsome woman has to do what a woman has to do. Savannah can be too small for certain types of things. If you want to go, it will be with my and your papa's blessing. And if you don't want to go, well, that will be with our blessing, too."

❧

THE FIRST THING Cora noticed when she stepped off the stage in Parsons Gulch was that everyone in the near vicinity stopped and stared at her.

The second thing she noticed was that everyone in the near vicinity was male.

The third thing she noticed was that the stares were appreciative.

And the fourth she noticed was that Aunt Lucille wasn't there to meet her.

Not surprising. Cora was five days later than her expected arrival because the train, due to a breakdown, had been two days late getting into Kansas City, which made her three days late to catch the stage which was to take her to wherever it was she was to catch the next stage to Parsons Gulch.

She was tired. She was covered in dust; dust that was probably turning to mud at her armpits because she was also miserably hot. Two days ago, at a stage stop, she'd removed her bustle and all but one of her petticoats so that now her traveling dress had no shape at all and its hem dragged the ground. She was pretty sure she was a bedraggled mess.

Turning, she watched as the stagecoach driver unloaded her trunk, and when she turned back to face the town again, she found herself facing a crowd of men that all but surrounded her. Unnerved, she swallowed.

The mass of men moved a little closer. When one of them

removed his hat, the rest of them snatched theirs off, too. No one spoke.

Cora didn't know if she was being worshipped or if they were about to burn her as a witch. She opened her mouth to say something – anything – but couldn't think of a thing to say.

Finally, one of the men stepped forward. "Can I escort you to wherever you want to go, ma'am?" and he crooked an elbow in invitation.

"Um, thank you," Cora replied, "but I expect my aunt will be along any minute now."

The man was missing a front tooth and had tobacco stains down his scraggly beard. He frowned. "Your aunt?"

"Yes. Uh, Lucille Manning?" Cora, who'd never in her life been the focus of so much male attention, felt herself beginning to panic.

"Oh, Miz Lucy," the man said with a wide smile. "The assay office has been real busy today. Guess she didn't hear the stage come in. I'll be glad to take you there, ma'am," and again he crooked his elbow.

"All-all right."

Immediately, elbowing several others so as to get there first, another man picked up her trunk, and another dove in to pick up her smaller valise, both men grinning from ear to ear and looking at her expectantly.

"Th-thank you," she murmured.

"My name's Abe," one said, the man who had her trunk resting on one shoulder.

"I'm Luke," the man holding her valise chimed in.

Cora blinked. "Uh, glad to meet you both," she replied.

"Hear that, Luke? She's glad to meet us. We're shore glad to meet you, too, Miss…. That is, Miz…?"

"Watley," Cora replied after a surprised moment. Was

everyone in Parsons Gulch so forward? "I'm, er, Miss Cora Watley."

"Don't mind them, Miss Cora," her escort said, glaring at her two luggage bearers before leading her over the planks that served as a makeshift walkway, the crowd of men following behind. "They ain't got no manners. I'm Gustaphus Cramer, but you can call me Gus."

"I'm Ben, ma'am," someone in the crowd behind called out. "I'm Grady, Miss Cora." "I'm Sol." "I'm Lester."

Gus turned his head to glare at the crowd behind them. "Shaddup, you ninnies. Cain't you see the lady's trying to walk here. This ain't the time for personal introductions." He turned back to grin up at her, being that she was a good head taller than he. "Sorry about that, ma'am."

Cora tuned her head and gave the crowd a small shy smile before turning back again. "It's quite all right, Mr. Cramer. I'm sure the gentlemen were just being polite to a stranger."

"Hear that?" someone behind whispered loudly. "She says we're polite."

"She's a pretty thing, ain't she?" someone else whispered.

"Pretty is as pretty does," another said, but this man didn't bother to keep his voice down. Neither did he sound all that complimentary.

Cora stiffened, but she'd known this was too good to last. She'd been a novelty, that's all. Whoever had spoken back there had seen her for what she was – tall, plainly made, and with the Watley nose.

But now they'd stopped in front of a wooden building with a crudely lettered sign above the door declaring 'Assay Office' and Mr. Cramer was leading her inside.

"Cora!" a feminine voice rang out. "Oh, my dear, I'm so sorry I wasn't there to meet you. I didn't hear the stage," and Cora was enveloped in a warm hug smelling of lavender and dust. Later Cora was to learn that everything and everyone in Parsons Gulch smelled slightly of dust.

Aunt Lucille took the men immediately in charge. "Thank you for bringing her to me, Gus. And Luke and Abe, thank you for bringing her luggage. Shoo now, all of you. My niece is here to stay a while so there will be plenty of time for you to get acquainted later. For now, Cora is tired and needs a good cup of tea."

"Hear that?" someone said reverently. "She needs a cup of tea."

"Oh, good lord. Let's go, Jake. The show's over."

This was the cynical voice Cora had heard before. She tried to see who it belonged to but the mass of men were already heading out the door of the small office, most of them dressed alike with collarless work shirts, suspenders or belts or even an extra bit of rope holding up rough canvas trousers tucked into heavy utilitarian boots. Most were hairy with beards of various colors and lengths.

In moments, the escort crowd was gone, leaving only the men doing business in the office to gaze at Cora in appreciative silence.

Aunt Lucille wasted no time hustling her through a back curtain and into the living quarters behind the office. She seated Cora in a rocking chair, placed a small tapestried footstool beneath her feet, put water on for tea, then sat down herself and folded her hands, her brown eyes sparkling.

"Now, dear, tell me all about the family and your trip out here, and I will tell *you* all about Parsons Gulch. I can hardly wait to see you take it by storm."

IF CORA HAD any doubts about taking the town by storm – and she did, lots of them – she didn't have them long.

The next morning, she and Aunt Lucille walked down the way to call on Mrs. Hawley, the mercantile owner's wife. They'd no sooner stepped out the door of the assay office than what had been a near empty street suddenly had men rounding corners, stepping off porches, and seeming to emerge from the dusty street itself, most immediately removing their hats.

Aunt Lucille laughed softly. "Welcome to Parsons Gulch, Cora."

"Goodness," Cora whispered. "Does this happen to you every time you go out?"

"Heavenly days, no. The men are always polite, of course, but I'm neither young nor unattached. You, on the other hand …." And she laughed again.

"Definitely not young," Cora replied gloomily, "but certainly unattached. And, with the Watley nose, likely to stay that way. You're Papa's sister. How did you escape it?"

"Some in the family get it, some don't," Aunt Lucille began, but was interrupted when one of the men in the near vicinity called out to them.

"Good morning, Miz Lucy, Miss Cora," and he presented the women with a small half bow, holding his hat over his heart.

Aunt Lucille acknowledged it with a smile and a regal nod. "Good morning," she replied, and gave Cora an unobtrusive poke with her elbow.

"Um, good morning," Cora said in her turn, not used to being greeted by complete strangers on the street. Such was just not done in Savannah. "Aunt Lucile, do you know that man?" she whispered as they passed on.

"Never saw him before in my life," her aunt answered cheerfully, "but I'm sure we'll be seeing him again. Forget Savannah etiquette, my dear. You're a sensation here. Enjoy it. And as for staying unattached, only if you choose to, Cora. Only if that's what you really want."

And so it was that they made their way down the street through a chorus of "Good mornings," "Howdy, ma'ams," a few "Buenos diases," a couple of "Bonjours," even one "Guten morgen," not a single greeting uttered without a hat removal and a worshipful gaze in Cora's direction.

Well, there was *one*.

He was tall, taller than Cora even; he didn't have a beard but sported a pencil thin mustache above a thin-lipped mouth that didn't smile. No canvas pants and work boots for this man. His clothing was of the finest broadcloth and his boots of hand-tooled leather. Nor did he remove his fine felt hat. It was pushed to the back of his head, doing nothing to shade cynical eyes the color of ancient gold coins.

He watched the ladies pass without saying a word.

"Who was that?" Cora whispered, once they were past the man's cold golden gaze and out of earshot.

"Spencer Callaway," Aunt Lucille told her. "He owns the Painted Jade saloon."

"Goodness," Cora said.

To which her aunt replied tartly, "If so, it's hard to find where Spencer Callaway is concerned. He never smiles and acts like he owns the town. Which, some say, he does."

There were no customers in the mercantile when they entered. Mrs. Hawley stood behind the counter sorting receipts, but when the bell jangled and she looked up to see them, she beamed. "Welcome, welcome. You must be Cora. Lucy has told me so much about you." Hardly taking a breath, she hollered, "Pa, get out here and mind the store. I've got company!"

Within moments, Cora and Lucille were in the Hawley's living quarters where that lady plied Cora with coffee cake and endless questions. Both her aunt and Mrs. Hawley were starved for news of the latest fashions, the latest parlor games, the latest forms of feminine crafts and handwork. Cora, who at twenty-eight was neither young nor old and for years had felt out of step with the majority of her sex, suddenly found herself viewed as an authority on modern womanly pursuits. It was a heady feeling.

So was the feeling she had when, an hour later, she and her aunt left the Hawley living quarters to walk through the store on their way back to the assay office and found the store a beehive of commerce, packed full of men looking over the goods and buying everything from bullets to beans.

Hats came off the moment the women appeared from the back reaches and the good mornings began all over again.

"Oh, for heaven's sake," Aunt Lucile exclaimed. "Good *morning*, all of you. Now let us pass. Mr. Manning's waiting for me. Cora's not going anywhere for a while. She'll be around," and she hustled her niece out the door. But not before someone thrust a small packet of lemon drops in Cora's hand – she didn't see who – and someone else startled her by handing her a licorice whip. Once out of the store, she also found herself holding a can of tomatoes.

Walking beside the befuddled girl, Lucille laughed all the way back to the assay office.

◈

THERE WASN'T a lot for a woman to do in Parsons Gulch; that is, if the woman was single. Aunt Lucille helped her husband, and Mrs. Hawley helped her husband, but Cora had no one to help except her aunt, which she did as much as possible. She took over the cooking and housekeeping chores, but in the small confines of the two room living quarters – Cora slept on the small sofa -- there wasn't much house to keep. As to cooking, with the limited ingredients available in Parsons Gulch, the meals tended to get repetitive.

With so few women in town, Cora's social life was limited as well. She was still a sensation every time she appeared outside the assay office, but she was finally getting used to it, even recognizing some of the men and conversing a bit with one or another of them as she walked down the street on her various errands when her aunt wasn't with her.

Invariably, one of the men would ask her to marry him, and invariably, Cora would smile and tell the man she wasn't ready to marry yet. Coming from a society where no man in her life had ever asked for her hand in marriage, let alone on a public street, now she was asked at least twice a day.

Every evening she was courted. Aunt Lucille, however, limited the swains to no more than three at a time and none on Friday or Saturday evenings when the four saloons were full and rowdiness the order of the night. But Sunday through Thursday nights would find three gentlemen, all washed up, slicked down, and wearing their cleanest shirts, sitting in the corner arrangement of the living area that designated the Manning's front parlor, drinking coffee from an honest to goodness cup and saucer and trying to carry on a conversation without dropping too many curse words.

The callers usually came bearing a small gift: a bit of hard candy in a twist of paper, a carefully copied out poem … sometimes original, sometimes not … a small gold nugget, a piece of ribbon. Once, even a tattered much worn copy of *Aesop's Fables*.

At first Cora tried to refuse these gifts till her aunt took her in hand. "Take them," she said. "These men are lonely. They not only want a wife, they want the civilization of courtship, to be on their best behavior and know that a woman is pleased with them. Their little gifts are to honor you, my dear, the same way a man would bring you flowers or candy in Savannah. Flowers and chocolates simply can't be had out here, so they're giving you the beauty and sweet-meats available to them. Don't deny them their efforts."

As for Cora, she'd never been so popular nor felt so beautiful.

Except, that is, on those rare occasions when she happened to encounter Spencer Callaway on the street and he leveled on her his unsmiling gaze, his cold golden eyes passing over her from the top of her head to the boots on her feet. That's when she remembered she bore the Watley nose that stripped her of any trace of feminine appeal.

She'd lift her head, raise her chin and pretend he didn't exist as she continued on her way on the arm of whatever man was escorting her at the moment, but in her heart of hearts she knew he did exist and that he found her lacking.

"There's to be a dance," Aunt Lucille announced one morning, coming into the living quarters from the assay office. "Won't it be fun? We haven't had one in ages."

Cora looked up from stirring the beans. "A dance? With so few women?"

Her aunt laughed. "Oh, we'll manage. You'll see. Spencer Callaway is holding it at the Painted Jade."

Shocked, Cora gazed at her open-mouthed. "Aunt Lucille! What will people say?" she finally managed.

And her aunt laughed again. "They'll say all kinds of things because everybody in town will be there. The Painted Jade is the only place big enough to have a decent sized dance floor and Spence owns the only piano in a hundred miles."

"Goodness," Cora said, still shocked, but also a bit thrilled. She'd never been in a saloon. "Don't tell my mama."

That Saturday night all the saloons in town closed for the dance at the Painted Jade. All liquor was locked away and an innocuous punch made by Mrs. Hawley took its place. If later in the evening, that punch took on a more interesting flavor, no one appeared to notice.

There was plenty of dancing and Cora discovered how it was managed with such a shortage of women. Half the men wore towels tied like an apron around their waists. These were the 'girls.' The men without the towels were the 'boys.' Periodically they traded places. One of Spencer's employees manned the piano and Cora found out Gus could play the violin. He played it quite well, too, so that sometimes the instrument was full of all the joy and sass of a fiddle, with everyone, including the women, whooping and stomping the steps of the country music, and sometimes it held all the dreamy romanticism of a violin, so that the dancers quietened down. At such times, even though the men danced with each other, one could almost feel the yearning for a life the frontier town of Parsons Gulch just didn't have.

Cora never lacked for a partner and she'd never had so much fun. Not a single one of her many partners danced with her out of duty. She wasn't the only belle of the ball, however. All of the three women were. None of them missed a dance unless they deliberately sat one out to catch their breath.

Gus was playing an especially evocative violin piece when, by unspoken consent, the men yielded the music to the only real couples in town. Aunt Lucille and Uncle Richard took the floor, as did Mr. and Mrs. Hawley, leaving Cora sitting on the sidelines to watch them, that old Savannah feeling creeping up her straight backbone. Then Spencer Callaway was before her, and without asking, led her onto the dance floor. She wasn't surprised to find he was a good dancer, but so was she. They didn't speak, Cora determined not to be the first to open her mouth.

When the music ended, he took her back where he'd

found her and disappeared into the crowd. She didn't see him again for the rest of the evening.

THOUGH SHE'D COME west with the hope of marriage, Cora found she wasn't in such a hurry after all. She thoroughly enjoyed the attention the men of Parsons Gulch lavished on her – save one, of course. These men didn't seem to notice her lack of classic beauty; they simply saw her as female to their male. She was good enough just as she was.

And she was gaining a new perspective on the men who surrounded her, too. They'd come west looking for something just as she had, only for them that something was wealth, or a do-over, or an escape from who-knew-what. But in their search, they, too, found they wanted the comfort of a helpmeet, a woman to make life easier for themselves, but most of all to form a unit for sharing both the joys and tribulations of this place far from the civilizations of their origins, and to keep the lonelies at bay.

Which was all well and good until there came the evening when, instead of the usual three, only one gentleman caller showed up to sit on Aunt Lucille's settee, drink coffee, and make stilted conversation while Cora smiled and asked him about the family he'd left behind in Norway. Instead of answering, he grew quiet, red-faced, and twitchy. He didn't finish his coffee and he didn't stay the usual forty-five minutes, but soon made a hurried excuse to leave.

The next morning, as she made her way to the mercantile, neither did there seem to be the usual crowd to tip their hats and wish her a good morning. Even Sam's courtly bow was missing. He merely lifted his hand and gave her a half-hearted wave before turning away and hurrying around the corner.

Cora sighed. Her new had apparently worn off. She was back to being the woman with the Watley nose and fast approaching spinsterhood. Probably, she should have settled on one of the men while she had the chance instead of prolonging the joy of her one shot at popularity.

At the mercantile, Mrs. Hawley seemed jittery and harried, filling Cora's order while telling her that Mr. Hawley wasn't well and that she was closing the store for the day to take care of him just as soon as Cora left.

Taking the hint, Cora didn't linger.

Back on the street, where before four men at least would have leapt to carry her packages, there were none. Jake went to tip his hat to her, however, but when he did, he almost tripped over his own two feet and had to lean against a post to get his bearings.

Well, of all things! Was the man drunk at this hour of the morning?

Disheartened, Cora returned to the assay office.

There were no customers nor was Aunt Lucille manning the counter. When Cora passed through the curtain to the living quarters, she heard the sound of retching coming from her aunt and uncle's bedroom, but in moments Aunt Lucile entered the kitchen area. "Richard isn't well, she said. "I think he's eaten something that doesn't agree with him, though I don't know what it could be. I'm fine, but how about you, Cora? Are you feeling all right?"

"Yes, I'm fine as well, Aunt. Don't worry about me, but Mr. Hawley is sick, too. Mrs. Hawley has closed the mercantile so she can care for him."

"A good idea. Lock the front door, please, Cora. If Mr. Hawley has the same illness as Richard, perhaps it's something else instead of just poor digestion. Parsons Gulch has no doctor. Are others ill, do you know?"

"I-I don't know. But there weren't many people on the

street today and those who were didn't seem … quite them-selves." Cora didn't want to discuss her feeling of humiliation and thinking only of herself this morning. "I-I thought Jake was drunk, but perhaps he was sick, too."

"Possibly," her aunt replied. "But I think it's best to stay indoors today. You will be all right on your own, won't you?"

"Of course. What can I do to help?"

"Nothing, my dear," her aunt replied, clearly distracted by the unpleasant sounds coming from the bedroom and already hurrying toward it to do whatever mysterious things she must do for her ailing husband.

All that day and the next Cora did little but make a weak tea for her uncle that he could not keep down and a stronger cup for her aunt to sip on when she could take a break from sick room duties. She also made a thin broth soup for her uncle, but he couldn't keep that down, either. Her aunt was exhausted but would not allow Cora to help in the sick room, telling her there was nothing a young unmarried girl should be doing in there.

And so Cora passed the time alone. For something to do she went through her aunt's work basket and mended every-thing in it needing mending. She finished embroidering her aunt's and uncle's initials on the matching handkerchiefs she planned to give them for Christmas, still two months away. She read *Aesop's Fables* from cover to cover and reread the poems, both the good and the bad, that had been given to her by her erstwhile beaus. With her aunt always in the sick room, there was no one to talk to.

When she looked out the front window in the assay office, she saw no one on the street, no sign of life anywhere. Parsons Gulch might have been a ghost town.

Finally, in desperation, the next time her aunt entered the kitchen area Cora told her she was going for a walk. The streets were empty, she would come to no harm. Too tired to argue, Aunt Lucille simply nodded her head and drank the more robust tea Cora had made for her.

Once out of doors Cora took a deep breath of cool fresh air. Both the assay office and the living quarters had smelled of the unpleasantries of illness in this particular form. But outdoors, the light breeze smelled only of the dust it stirred up in the street. Certainly, there was nothing else to stir up the dust; no horses or mules or wagons. No people.

Had everyone left as she and her family were cloistered in the assay office, Cora wondered. All of the town's few buildings were closed, shuttered, and lifeless.

That is, all but the Painted Jade saloon. The heavy wooden door behind the bat-winged entrance stood open. Slowly, Cora began to walk in that direction, her boots sounding overly loud on the wood plank walkway in the town's silence.

It seemed scandalous to have a saloon as her destination, but she'd been there for the town dance, she rationalized, so no one should object if she peeked in its doorway now.

But she hadn't reached the door before she smelled the same stench that permeated the assay office and was still several steps away when she heard the first moans. Cautiously pushing open one of the swinging doors, she looked inside. Her jaw dropped.

Cots took up most of the floor, and where there was room for them on the not too clean floor were pallets. Every available space to lay one's head held a sick man, some lying quietly, some writhing and holding their belly. The smell of vomit and diarrhea was overpowering. Covering her mouth and nose, Cora stared wide-eyed.

"What the hell do you want?"

Startled, Cora's gaze shifted off to her far right where she saw Spencer Callaway standing beside a cot, a bucket in one hand, a wet rag in the other. But it was a Spencer she'd never seen before. His thin mustache was ragged and unkempt, his chin and jaws covered with several days' stubble. It was the first time she'd seen him without a coat, too, and his once white shirt was stained and open at the throat without its usual collar. He'd rolled his sleeves to the elbows and his black pants were splattered with things she didn't want to identify.

Still, though seemingly sunken behind dark rings of tiredness, Spencer's gold coin eyes managed to look right down into Cora's shortcomings.

"I-I wondered where everyone was," Cora said, just a bit afraid of him.

"Now you know. Now scram."

Her head snapped up, her chin jutted forward, and she gave him the slit-eyed Watley stare perfected by her papa and, like the patriarchal nose, passed on to Cora, before she turned on her heel and left, muttering to herself all the way back to the assay office.

Once there, she changed into her oldest dress, tied a rag around her hair, and on her way back out the door hollered to her aunt that she was helping some people down the street and didn't know when she would be back. Without waiting for her aunt's reply, she closed the door behind her.

Pushing through the batwing doors, the stench of illness immediately slapped her in the face, but she entered the saloon anyway.

Spencer looked up from trying to pour a little liquid down a reluctant throat and scowled. "What are you doing back here? I told you to scram."

"So you did," Cora replied. "Where are you emptying the slops?"

He gave her a long hard look, probably not as long or as hard as he would have liked because he swayed on his feet. "I'll show you," he said.

When she asked, he also showed her where the mop was and where the saloon's small kitchen was. And then he went back to doing what he'd been doing – washing hands and faces, holding a bucket while some poor soul spewed his insides into it, shouldering another as he made his weak way to the back outhouse and cleaning up after him if the man couldn't make it that far. He also ignored her completely.

Cora mopped when she could find the time, lugged nasty bedding to the Chinese laundry, often retrieving it before it was completely dry but needed anyway, apologizing as the Asian women fussed. Spencer put his foot down on outhouse duty, and she gladly let him have his way, but she washed hands and faces and held buckets, coaxed fluids down throats and hoped they wouldn't exit again in either direction. She made weak tea and rich chicken soup for those who could handle it and a thinner one for those who could manage but a swallow or two.

Where Spencer had found a chicken, she didn't know and didn't ask. She'd have bet there wasn't a chicken within two hundred miles of Parsons Gulch, but if she had, she'd have lost her money.

Cora, who never in her life had seen a male less than fully clothed, not even her father and brothers, now learned all about a man's anatomy. Shocked at first, it didn't take her long to get over it. For one thing, she had no time for titillation; for another, she was just too tired to be amazed.

She sang and teased, murmured soothing nonsense, and nagged and cajoled her patients into trying to get better. And, at last, most did, though they lost three of them.

Late in the evening of the third day, Cora and Spencer found themselves leaning side by side and shoulder to shoulder against a side wall. They were afraid to sit down, afraid they'd fall asleep if they did. But leaning against the wall, they could catnap.

"What caused this, do you know?" Cora asked, without opening her eyes. "None of the women got sick. The Chinese didn't get sick. *You* didn't get sick."

"I have no idea," Spencer answered tiredly. "But at a guess, I'd say it was bad whiskey."

Cora's eyes popped open. "You served bad whiskey!"

"Not intentionally, no," he replied stiffly, and turned his head to give her a glare. "I'll remind you there are four saloons in this town, but we all bought stock from the same source a few days ago. There's been Indian trouble up the trail and not much was getting through. We were all running low."

"So why didn't you get sick?"

"I don't drink rotgut. Like most saloon owners, I drink very little, but when I do, I want the good stuff, not stuff made three days ago of unknown ingredients and in a dirty barrel. Usually, it doesn't matter much, but this time apparently it did."

"Umm," Cora said sleepily, and went back to her dozing.

After another twenty minutes or so, she straightened, not sure what had awakened her. And then it dawned on her. Except for a few snores, the room was silent. No retching, no bodily gurgles. Beside her, Spencer still leaned against the wall, breathing quietly, his eyes closed. It amazed Cora that he still managed to stay upright. He'd been at this days longer than she, and she was exhausted.

Looking around, she spotted an empty cot, probably from one of the deceased occupants, but beggars couldn't be choosers. Reaching out, Cora took Spencer's arm. "Spence," she said, "I see an empty cot. I want you in it."

"Huh? What?" he mumbled, wiping a hand over his face.

"Cot. You. Sleep," she said. "Let's go," and she took his forearm in an iron grip and led him to it.

"No. You," he protested, still dazed.

"I'll wake you later. Then it will be my turn. Lie down."

"I'm not your dog, Cora."

She laughed. "Maybe not, but you will obey me in this."

And he did. But before she could move away, he took her hand. "Pretty is as pretty does," he said, and smiled.

That smile was the nail in her coffin. Cora's heart did a crazy jiggle and she knew it would never beat the same way again. She also knew the source of that hateful comment when she'd first arrived in Parsons Gulch.

"Huh," she said, but Spencer was already asleep and still holding her hand. He was also still smiling. Slowly Cora pulled her hand from his flaccid grip but stood for a moment to look down at his sleeping face.

"Huh," she whispered to herself, and she, too, smiled.

She never did wake him, but Spencer woke himself several hours later and insisted she take the cot. When she awoke, bright sunshine poured through the saloon's open door and the others on the cots were beginning to stir. Not with illness now, but with the urge to be gone and about their business.

One by one, they left the premises, every man shaking Spencer's hand, every man thanking Cora profusely.

A week later, Spencer and Cora were married. The whole town attended the wedding. There was music and laughter and dancing and punch. This time, no one spiked it. Whiskey might have been available in the back alley, but many of the men had decided to go on the wagon, at least for a while.

Spencer changed the name of his saloon, renaming it The Pretty Does. An itinerant artist painted a portrait of Cora … fully clothed, to her secret disappointment. Her husband proudly hung it behind the bar.

It's said a cowboy once came into the saloon, eyed the portrait, and sneered, "The Pretty Does, huh? Why, that gal ain't pretty. With that schnoz, she's …."

He stopped suddenly, turning pale.

At least twenty guns were pointed right at his midsection. Even the bartender had pulled out a shotgun.

The cowboy cleared his throat. "Uh, what I was about to say, boys," he managed, his face now a bright red, "is the drinks are on me. Let's drink to the prettiest gal in Parsons Gulch!"

MISS LILLY

"In the new code of laws which I suppose it will be necessary for you to make I desire you would remember the ladies, and be more generous and favorable to them than your ancestors. Do not put such unlimited power into the hands of the husbands. Remember all men would be tyrants if they could. If particular care and attention is not paid to the ladies we are determined to foment a rebellion, and will not hold ourselves bound by any laws in which we have no voice, or representation."

Abigail Adams
    Letter to John Adams (March 31, 1776)

MISS LILLY

THIS IS A STORY MY GRAMMAW TOLD ME ABOUT OLD MCELROY township, back in the days when it was known as Suggens Crossing. It was a raw, rip-roaring town back then, she said, and a time when individuals had more clout than law and order. Oh, it had a sheriff all right, but he listened to the will of the people more than he scoured through law books. It was the people who elected him and, rightly or wrongly, it was the people he answered to.

Events that happened back then, Grammaw said, couldn't happen today. Again, rightly or wrongly.

So, as my grammaw told it, here's the story of Miss Lilly, a longtime resident. You're sure to recognize the name since the town library is named for her. I'll leave it to you to decide if things played out as they should.

JOHN BAILEY JR. might have been born in a dirt floor cabin, but he didn't live in it past his tenth birthday. By then his daddy had founded Suggens Crossing's only bank and it had thrived. Nobody was sure how John Senior put the money together to do it, but in those days folks didn't ask a whole lot of questions, nor did they stay around long enough to get answers even if they did.

Suggens Crossing was just that, a place where two main trails crossed in some of the meanest country travelers had to go through; people from the east headed west, mostly, full of dreams involving the gold fields and opportunity. But there was also to-ing and fro-ing from points north and south with goods coming from or going to Mexico.

I imagine the first building set up at the crossing was a makeshift saloon, probably by a man named Suggens, but nobody knows for sure. From that one saloon gradually came all the rest. Once stopped to wet their whistle, travelers found the Crossing a good place to renew supplies, rest or trade for fresh pack animals, or just take a breather their own self before heading on toward wherever their goal was taking them.

So, a lot of just passing through Suggens Crossing there at first, but those who decided to stay found opportunity and a modest amount of wealth right here in our dusty little high desert town. It might not have looked like much at the time, but after a couple of years it had added another three or four saloons, a general store, a smithy, a bath house ... and John Senior's bank.

Ol' John Bailey always said Suggens Crossing would be an important metropolis some day and to that end, he went on to build himself the fanciest house he could imagine. In a town where most of the few families who lived there lived either behind or above their businesses, you couldn't miss it. Just down what was by then called Main Street and sitting on a couple of acres of catclaw, cactus, and scrub juniper, the house had two stories, five bedrooms, a front parlor and a back parlor, and a big wraparound porch with curly trim in the corners. John put up a black iron fence around the property to keep out the cows and the drunk cowboys from the ranches that developed as the town grew, then he added a wide curving drive with a fancy gate for any carriages he anticipated would come calling someday.

It was a lot of house for just himself, his wife, and his boy, but ol' John also anticipated having more children. Unfortunately, his wife died having their stillborn daughter. They say her death took a lot out of him, what with just himself and his boy rattling around in a house that now felt like a coat three sizes too big.

John never remarried. And he stayed out of the house as much as he could, the story goes, handling his grief by turning his attention to his bank and indulging his only son. John Junior rode the best horses, wore the best clothes, and seemed to thrive on tearing up or tearing into any and everything. John patiently paid for the mischief his son caused. Boys will be boys, he told anyone who complained. But when he had to pay out for all the full bottles of good liquor Junior shot off the back wall in the new hotel's fancy bar, as well as pay for the extensive damages the boy did when he rode his horse into the hotel in the first place, John apparently decided enough was enough and sent the boy, now about fifteen, to relatives back east to finish his education and calm him down some.

It seemed to work. Junior would come home a couple of times a year, a little taller and a little more handsome each visit. His wild days were over, it appeared. He never stayed long, though, and didn't have much good to say about the town of his birth when he was here, even though, true to his daddy's predictions, Suggens Crossing was growing both in population and prestige. With statehood on the horizon, there was even talk of it becoming a county seat.

But as Junior grew into manhood, it was obvious to all that John Senior and John Junior couldn't be more different.

Senior might be the richest man in town, but he was still the man who started a bank with the change in his pockets – or however it was he started his bank. His clothes were the same comfortable style he'd worn for twenty years, his boots the scuffed utilitarian footwear of the working man, and he ended all his transactions with a handshake and a slap on the back. If they involved an old friend, they also included a glass of the good stuff.

Junior, now, seldom set foot in the bank when he was home, wore suits from back east clearly tailored to fit, and he never wore boots, but shoes … highly polished, of course. His hat was a derby. If the town hadn't known he was born and half-raised in Suggens Crossing, folks might have thought he was a tenderfoot. He didn't seem to recognize any of the old friends he used to pal around with, either.

And, by the way, don't call him Junior. He was John. Not Johnny. John. When it was pointed out to him that two John Baileys in town led to confusion, the person doing the pointing was told flatly to deal with it. The way the town chose to deal with it was to call him Junior behind his back, usually with a derogatory chuckle.

As Junior got older, his visits slowed to once a year, but it had been three years since he'd been home when his father died. As the only child, Junior inherited the bank and was smart enough to realize that the bank, the source of his income, couldn't run itself, especially in a western town only recently turned civilized.

Junior didn't return home alone to lay his daddy to rest and take over his inheritance. He brought a new bride with him.

The town had been expecting him, so no one paid much attention when he stepped off the train and looked around with a slight derisive curl to his lip. But when he then turned to hand down a smiling girl who looked like the first flower of spring, the whole town seemed to take a collective breath. All activity on the station platform came to a sudden halt.

Junior beamed, as well he should.

Miss Lilly, as the town came to call her, put up her parasol, tucked a dainty hand into the crook of his arm, and the two of them proceeded to stroll down the only walkway in town, the one lining Main Street and leading to the Bailey homeplace, where it came to an end. The couple was followed by a small negro maid who didn't look a day over sixteen but who held her head high and proud and gazed neither left nor right as she trailed behind her mistress.

But Miss Lilly looked. You could tell she was fascinated by the town and found pleasure in what she saw. Her smile was genuine as she nodded to the men doffing their hats when the couple passed by and was just as open and friendly toward the women, the women half-smiling themselves as they examined everything Miss Lilly wore, from the confection of a hat to the small bustle defining her gauzy day dress.

At one point, Junior leaned down and said something quietly to her, and someone heard her reply with a light tinkling laugh, "But John, everyone is being so polite and friendly. Why should I not be friendly back? After all, this is my home now." And she gave him a quick kiss on the cheek.

He patted the small hand still tucked into his arm and they moved on, but it was noted that Junior's ears turned red and his mouth thinned grim. The town, however, was enchanted. Not only by the woman's loveliness but by her accent. It wasn't southern, or eastern, and certainly not western, but something rich and full and exotically strange that went right down to the toes and curled up again. As some were wont to say, they could listen to her talk all day.

The couple hired Agatha Hislop as a cook-housekeeper, and it was Aggie who more or less kept the town informed as to the goings on in the Bailey household. Aggie went to her own home at night, so her reporting was mainly on how nice Miss Lilly was to work for since Junior spent his days at the bank. Even when he was home, he barely gave Aggie the time of day, so she said.

And she said Susan, the maid, was a sweet little thing and obviously loved her mistress. And her mistress obviously loved her back, the two of them, mistress and maid, laughing and chatting together as they became accustomed to their new home. That is, when Junior wasn't there. When he was there, all laughter between the two young women stopped, Susan becoming silently attentive and Miss Lilly completely ignoring her except to give an order.

Junior called the maid Sukey the few times he stooped to address her. And, Aggie reported, Aggie was to call him Mister John, even though he'd been best pals with her son, Sam, when he was a boy and she'd more than once chased the two boys out of her house with a threatening broom when they got too rowdy.

Even though the Baileys were the closest thing Suggens Crossing had to high society and Junior had the airs to prove it, the town admired Miss Lilly as one of its own. She had a kind word for everyone, stopping to chat with the ladies at the general store or after church, even when Junior would have hustled her away.

She was a bright light in our grey desert town, gifting us with her laughter and high fashion and generous ways, because if the town had fallen in love with Miss Lilly, wonder of wonders, she had fallen in love back.

Like all lovers, the town put on its best face for her and was delighted when she recognized traits the town never knew it had. Where the town's folks once considered their lives filled with drudgery just to get by, she saw their hard work as making for themselves a better future, which was a wonderful goal. To her eyes, that dust and mud folks slogged through and complained about were simply paths leading to greater things. She looked at Suggens Crossing as one would look at an infant and see the promise of its possibilities. And because she saw these things, ultimately so did the town. Miss Lilly made it proud of what it was and what it was achieving.

Junior, on the other hand.... Well, let's just say, Junior held different views. Apparently, Miss Lilly wasn't conducting herself quite up to his standards.

He once told Jake Robbins that her family's money came from some kind of big plantation down in the Caribbean. She'd grown up there, he said, so she didn't have the better manners as practiced by society on the east coast. Jake had replied he thought her manners were charmin', but Junior had simply hiked an eyebrow and changed the subject. What did Jake, a simple cowhand, know? Only later, and quite by accident, did Junior learn that slow talking, charmin' Jake's family on his mother's side was one of those east coast brahmans Junior held in such high esteem.

After a while, it didn't take long for the town to notice that when Miss Lilly was out and about with Junior, her sparkle dimmed a bit and her greetings to others they happened to meet was a little more muted than they had been in the first few months of her arrival. By herself or when it was just her and Susan, she was as bright and vivacious as ever, but with Junior she was far more subdued.

For example, as Grammaw described it, this was Miss Lilly when she was alone greeting someone she knew on the street: "Why, Janie Tipton. How are you? And how is little Jimmy? Such a darling little boy and so clever!" And she and Miz Tipton would chat a while.

And this is Miss Lilly when she was with Junior, and only if the other party greeted her first: "Mrs. Tipton," with a small nod of her head and not much of a smile, and she and Junior would pass on.

See what I mean? The town, knowing Junior, put the onus on him for squashing her down. It was also noticed that Miss Lilly only invited the ladies for tea during the hours when Junior was at the bank and made sure the tea party was over before he arrived home.

Aggie, who made the little sandwiches and dainty cookies for the affair then joined the ladies herself, as did Susan. Aggie said Junior didn't know about those tea parties and word went around to make sure he never found out.

The town might delight in the harmless secrets it kept from the man, but everyone also knew that Junior's bank had the power to foreclose on their mortgages if they got so much as a week behind, and that he had the final yea or nay for anyone desperate enough to come in for a loan. Many a rancher or business owner depended on those loans to see them through unexpected lean times, so folks were understandably careful when they were around him. Some of the old-timers called him John to his face, but the rest of the town called him Mr. Bailey ... to his face. Only the most scared, desperate, and out of options called him Sir.

The women noticed it first, Grammaw said, how Miss Lilly's style seemed to change. The colors she wore became more muted, greys and mauves, instead of the pinks and blues and greens that became her so well. The dress styles themselves over time almost looked like they choked her they were so tight at the throat and at the wrists. Aggie told it that Junior insisted she be fashionable without flaunting herself, so not for Miss Lilly were the looser and more comfortable day dresses that the rest of the women wore.

Aggie also said that when she served the couple supper before she left for the evening that now Miss Lilly rarely spoke but kept her gaze on her plate except to quietly tell Aggie 'thank you' and 'please.'

One night she heard Junior tell his wife, "Lilly, I found you far too forward with Sheriff Nolan when we were out today."

And Miss Lilly replied, keeping her gaze lowered, "I'm sorry, John."

"Don't let it happen again, my dear," Junior said, cutting into his steak.

"No, John." And, according to Aggie, Miss Lilly seemed to give a little shiver.

When Aggie returned to the kitchen, Susan whispered, "All she did was say hello. She didn't even smile." The little maid had tears in her eyes.

The town raised its collective eyebrows, but you didn't go around interfering in another man's family business, so it held its peace, justifying itself with the knowledge that Aggie was a known gossip, even if the town loved to hear what she had to say.

Then came the incident when Miss Lilly hired Helen Jeffers to make her a new dress.

To take Miss Lilly's measurements for waist and hip size, she had Miss Lilly take off her skirt and took the measurements over her thin pantaloons. But when it came to taking the measurements needed for her upper torso, strangely Miss Lilly didn't want to remove her long-sleeved blouse. "But you're wearing a chemise," Helen was said to have argued.

Miss Lilly looked at her for a long moment, then said the oddest thing. "All right, but please don't tell my husband I did this. I fell, you see, and he might not be happy that you will have seen the bruises."

And there were bruises, over her back and her upper arms.

"That was quite a fall," Helen was said to have commented when she saw them.

After that, Miss Lilly sent her measurements back east and ordered from a dressmaker there.

There was the time Miss Lilly missed church two Sundays in a row. She wasn't feeling well, Junior told anyone who asked. The churchgoers guessed that she might be in the family way. But when someone asked Aggie, she said she wasn't sure, that when she'd arrived for work that Saturday morning, Miss Lilly was still abed and made no appearance downstairs at all. She said the bedroom door remained closed and only Susan was allowed to take meals up to her and see to her needs. Susan wasn't talking but Aggie said the little maid was angry as bedamned.

Miss Lilly kept to her room for over two weeks and when she finally emerged, she was pale and thin. When Aggie asked what had ailed her, all she would say was, "Please, Aggie, don't ask. Let it go."

Later that week, Miss Lilly was spotted at the train station buying train tickets, Susan and her portmanteau beside her. But before the train arrived, Junior did. The ticket master said he took her upper arm real tight and squeezed. "Going somewhere, my dear?" he asked.

"I want to go home and visit my family for a while, John," she answered, lifting her head high, but her face had turned as pale as paper.

"Another time, darling," the ticket master said Junior replied. "Today you're going home to *my* home where you belong," and he marched her down the street back to the Bailey homestead.

Aggie reported that no one said a word at supper that night, but it was noted that apparently Miss Lilly had another one of her sick spells, remaining again in her room for an extended period of time and out of sight of everyone except her husband and Susan. Susan, raging and livid, but not talking.

Time went by and the periodic sick spells continued.

Then several people saw Miss Lilly climbing the stairs to Jesse Lovington's office, the town's only lawyer who kept an office over the general store. It was whispered about that she wanted to find out how to get a divorce.

The good citizens of Suggens Crossing gasped. In those days, a divorced woman was considered no better than she should be, the next thing to a prostitute according to some. Still, because of those suspicious sick spells, there was a certain amount of sympathy. Miss Lilly was their favorite daughter, after all, and Junior the oily banker.

Lovington never told what was discussed in his office, but he did mention that the bank held the mortgage to his ranch.

Whatever their conversation was about, nothing came of it. When there wasn't another of Miss Lilly's sick spells after her visit to the lawyer, the town breathed a sigh of relief. Apparently Junior never got wind of it, and the town wasn't about to tell him.

Those quiet suppers Aggie reported on finally got a little conversation. She heard Miss Lilly ask Junior if she couldn't have the grounds around the house 'landscaped,' as she called it. The way she phrased the request appealed to Junior's ambitions. "Back east," Miss Lilly said, "all the great homes have beautiful grounds. Don't you think our grounds should have a few trees, too, and flower beds? We could even import some plants from my home in the islands. They are so beautiful and no one out here has ever seen the like."

She kept her gaze downcast and took a dainty bite of her pudding.

Junior used a forefinger to smooth his mustache as he thought a moment. "You might be right, my dear. Trees and gardens would turn our home into a showplace. We have a good deep well to keep it all watered, so why not? With exotic flowers from the islands, people will come from all over just to see them." He smiled. "Put a list together of the plants you want, and I'll order them."

And that's how a little piece of the desert bloomed around the Bailey mansion. It's still there and a showplace, just as Junior said it would be.

It wasn't easy. Shoots and seeds, cuttings and trees arrived by train, were carefully nurtured, fenced and shaded, babied and coddled by Susan and Miss Lilly. The two of them were often seen puttering around the flower beds and practically begging the plants there to stay healthy and thrive in the dry desert heat. Some of the plants were familiar to the town and some had never been seen before. Some were flowering plants, and some were not.

A few of the more unassuming plants, Susan told Aggie, made excellent drinkable teas that were good for numerous aches and pains. Among other things. At the tea parties, Miss Lilly always had a variety of these herbal teas available for sampling as well as the much enjoyed imported orange pekoe.

Miss Lilly, being Miss Lilly, was generous with cuttings and root clusters from those flowers or bushes that could be propagated in such a manner and passed them on to any of the town's women who wanted them. Most of the women didn't have the water resources the Bailey mansion had but nurtured the treasured cuttings or roots in whatever pot or container they could find. It was noted that those plants that went to seed after they bloomed were planted near the iron fence bordering the Bailey residence. Anyone on the street side of the fence could reach through the bars and casually grab some if they so desired, and many did.

A woman's heart yearns for natural beauty, Grammaw said, and showed me a rose bush in her back yard that came from one of Miss Lilly's cuttings. It was covered with big fat pink roses, lush in their blooming. To this day, the smell of roses reminds me of my grammaw's house.

But, of course, there's always a fly in the ointment.

After Junior saw an old peach can on the front windowsill of the Cunningham place, Miss Lilly had another sick spell. The can had held a small struggling plant with a single courageous bloom. Apparently, Miss Lilly wasn't supposed to share.

"It just needed a little morning sun," Marjorie Cunningham said tearfully to anyone who would still speak to her.

It took Miss Lilly an extra long time to come out of her bedroom this time and when she finally did, her movements were slow and jerky. For a week, after Junior left for the day, Susan would take Miss Lilly to a rocking chair on the front porch to enjoy what was left of the morning cool and the smell of the roses that now bloomed around its perimeter. Then the maid went to the kitchen to brew up one of her medicinal teas for her mistress.

Folks often stopped by the front porch to visit for a little while, Grammaw said, and when they left, they were not happy at all with Miss Lilly's pallor or listless demeanor. The town worried.

But that's all it did. No one in Suggens Crossing was brave enough to confront Junior with the issue, especially when it was an issue that could not be proven but could only be speculated on.

Miss Lilly kept more and more to herself as she and Susan cultivated their ever-expanding garden. She didn't hand out anymore cuttings or starter plants, and those who'd already received such were careful to make sure they only bloomed in places where they could not be seen from the street.

There was some disappointment because of this, for among Miss Lilly's roses she'd also planted something with a gorgeous feathery deep purple bloom and blood red leaves that made a lovely contrast to the pinks, reds, yellows and whites of the roses themselves. No one had ever seen anything like these flowers. When asked what they were, Miss Lilly always gave the name, the syllables rolling off her tongue in that rich accent of hers. However, the name was so foreign the women could neither spell it nor even remember it once they left through the front gate. It had to be one of her exotic plants from the islands, they thought.

In the meantime, Junior began having a few sickly spells himself. It started with a cough, but coughs and sniffles usually went around Suggens Crossing that time of year, so neither he nor anyone else thought anything about it. Aggie suggested he try one of Susan's teas. It had helped her when she'd had the cough and sniffles, she said. So he had Susan brew one for him, and sure enough, after a few days he seemed to get better.

Then his joints began to hurt to the point it was painful for him to walk up the stairs or hold a pen. Rheumatism, Doc Perry said. Junior snorted. He was too young for rheumatism. When did a Suggens Crossing doctor know what he was talking about, anyway? The doc merely lifted an eyebrow, shrugged a shoulder, and muttered a few choice words after Junior stiffly walked out the door.

Again, Aggie suggested one of Susan's teas. And, again, the tea seemed to help. Junior's joints loosened up, the pain went away, and except for the tingling that had begun in his toes and fingertips, he was feeling his old self again. That was, until the tingling began to travel from his fingertips into his palms and from his toes to the soles and arches of his feet. The fancy cane he'd always affected became a necessity. And this time, Susan's teas didn't seem to be getting the job done.

Junior went back to the doctor. Doc Perry was the only doc in town at the time, and after poking and prodding around the vital spots and listening to Junior's chest, he told Junior he couldn't find anything wrong, except that his heartbeat seemed a little fast. (When this was recounted, some wag said the doc must have been hearing the seconds ticking on the wall clock because everyone knew Junior had no heart.) Still, without actually saying it, the doc gave Junior the impression the banker was suffering from nothing more than imaginary aches and pains. Junior left in a huff and said he was taking the train to San Antonio to get a second opinion.

He refused to take Miss Lilly with him, but while he was gone, she began to smile again.

All too soon, he returned. That city doctor hadn't found anything wrong, either. Of course, Junior didn't say that. When anyone asked, and few did, he simply said all doctors were quacks and he'd stick to Sukey's teas.

He did quit climbing the stairs, however, and had a bed brought down and set up in the back parlor. More and more he was dependent on his cane. On those days when he didn't make it to the bank, he made life miserable for everyone in the house, Aggie said. Susan took to making him teas that made him nap most of the day, though he often seemed to feel better afterward, enough that he would hobble down to the bank for a couple of hours in the afternoon and make life miserable for his employees there.

The tingling continued to climb, from his palms up his arms, from his feet up his legs. He began staying in his bed in the back parlor more and more. While Susan's teas helped him sleep, they didn't seem to help whatever it was causing the unpleasant tingling that was slowly turning into an out and out burning.

Junior was scared enough to have Susan go for the

doctor, quack or not. Doc Perry was stymied. He had Susan bring him samples of the various herbal teas she made but could find nothing he was unfamiliar with. He even had a cup of chamomile himself, sweetened with a little honey. While he was at the house, he decided to check on Miss Lilly, but Miss Lilly was looking better and better every day. Doc Perry privately put it down to Junior no longer climbing the stairs. "If your teas are working, keep making them for him," he told Susan before he left the house.

Susan smiled and nodded. "I'll do that, Doctor Perry," she promised.

As for Miss Lilly, she went back to having her tea parties for the ladies of the town even though Junior was always in the house now and could hear every word that was said. Nothing said was ever unkind. Actually, no one mentioned him at all. After the women left, however, he railed against the riff-raff being allowed into his house – into *his* house, dammit -- but bedridden as he was, he couldn't do much about it. "Wait till I get better, Lilly," he threatened, and now didn't seem to mind that Aggie heard him. "Then you'll be sorry and do what I say."

To which Miss Lilly always replied, "Yes, John." Only she didn't hang her head or keep her gaze on the floor.

The town kept tabs with what was going on and wondered about it. John Junior's illness took on the glamour of a good mystery story and they followed its installments week after week. Miss Lilly kept anyone who asked apprised of her husband's condition, and in church asked the pastor to pray for him. Which the preacher did, loudly and at length.

Whatever was wrong with Junior's body got worse. By now, he couldn't lift his head off the pillow. Susan's teas had no effect at all, but he seemed to think they did and constantly asked for them. He had to be helped to drink, though, and his meals had become broths and mashed vegetables, the only food he seemed able to swallow. Soon, too, he was unable to talk. Doc Perry came again and left again, as mystified as the rest of the town. He did not ask for a cup of tea for himself, however.

Inevitably, Junior breathed his last.

The whole town and surrounding area came to his funeral. He would have been proud at the size of it, probably seeing it as his due. Grammaw said it remained unclear whether the town folk came from relief or simply to enjoy the gathering. What *was* clear was that Junior would not be missed. Miss Lilly, Susan, and Aggie all wore black, of course. Turned out, it was a lovely sophisticated color against Miss Lilly's porcelain skin, and her hat, with its frothy netting and black silk flowers, was a sight to behold. She didn't have tears to shed, though she put a black silk handkerchief up to her lips several times during the service.

Junior was buried beside his father and mother in the Bailey family plot. His was a simple grave without a headstone, though Miss Lilly said that she was having one made. Junior had put up a tall obelisk for his father with the family name carved into it, so it was assumed that his headstone would be just as fancy when it was put in place.

With no children, Miss Lilly inherited everything – the house, some ranch land she hadn't known Junior possessed, a couple of rental houses, a saloon, and the bank. Thus, began a new financial era for Suggens Crossing. She was a canny one, Miss Lilly was, but also kind and generous. No one could put one over on her, but she could be understanding when life caused a late payment or demanded emergency loans.

And she remained generous, donating land for a park, seeing that trees were planted along Main Street – the ones you see there today. Front yards had and have as many flower beds as their owners' desire, and it doesn't matter where those flowers come from. Suggens Crossing became the vision Miss Lilly always saw in it, and its citizenry frequently patted itself on the back for its pride in the town, the library, the two churches, the new name.

'McElroy,' it's known by now. Grammaw wasn't sure where the new name came from, but all agreed it sounded a little more important than 'Suggens Crossing.'

After living with Junior, no one was surprised when Miss Lilly didn't remarry for several years. She and Susan and Aggie seemed to rock along just fine in the Bailey mansion, holding frequent tea parties and soirees open to anyone who wanted to come. Junior might never have lived.

But eventually Susan married, a cowboy who took her north where he was foreman on a ranch. And ultimately Aggie's husband wanted her to stay home with him during the day now that he'd retired and their children were grown and gone.

It took over a year before anyone noticed that the lovely purple flowers mixed in with the roses around the porch of the Bailey home were no longer there. When asked, Miss Lilly said they'd outgrown their usefulness, so she'd pulled them up and burned them.

Which made a few remember Susan's teas, though no one ever said anything.

Miss Lilly did remarry after a few years of living alone – to slow talkin' Jake Robbins who seemed to love the high desert west as much as she did. He could match her dollar for dollar, too, so it was a marriage of equals. They split their time between his ranch and her home in town and, by and by, five children came of their union.

It was after a funeral several years later when the sheriff and his wife wandered the cemetery, passing the time and idly reading the headstones. At one point, they strolled by the Bailey obelisk. Junior's headstone was there now, too, but small, about the size of a footstone. It didn't read John Allen

Bailey, Jr. as one would expect, either, nor did it have the dates of birth and death. It simply read, "Junior."

That's all. Just the one word.

The couple looked at each other. "What do you think?" the sheriff's wife asked him.

"I don't know," he replied. "And I don't want to know."

"What do you think, Grammaw?" I asked, knowing her story was over.

She touched my cheek and smiled at me. "I don't care to guess," she said. "But this I do know. No child or grandchild of mine will ever be called Junior."

LIFE IN THE WILD WEST WITH MRS. LAURA COSGROVE

A traveler has a right to relate and embellish his adventures as he pleases, and it is very impolite to refuse that deference and applause they deserve.

Rudolf Erich Raspe
Travels of Baron Munchausen (1785)

LIFE IN THE WILD WEST WITH
MRS. LAURA COSGROVE

SHE WAS IN LOVE.

With her new husband, so she said. With life, certainly.

But most of all, Laurie Cosgrove was in love with *adventure*.

Born and raised in the small farming community of Chittings, Kansas, the farthest afield she'd ever been was a visit to an aunt in Middle Falls, thirty miles away. Middle Falls wasn't much larger than Chittings, and to the young Laurie it could have been her hometown's mirror image – a bitter disappointment to a girl who for weeks had looked forward to seeing something *different*.

Her new husband, Caleb Cosgrove had a good head on his shoulders, according to Laurie's parents, who thought his steadying influence might be good for their daughter. Laurie had known him all her life. Their families were close, living on adjacent farms on the outskirts of Chittings. They knew the same people, shopped in the same stores, went to the same church on Sundays.

As a younger son, Caleb had known he would have to

move on someday if he ever wanted a family of his own. His parents' farm could sustain no more than two families at a time and it was a foregone conclusion those two families would be his parents and that of his older brother, now married and with one child, another on the way. The bedrooms in the farmhouse were full. It was time for Caleb to go.

He was ready. A year ago, he'd headed west to seek land he could get cheaply if one was willing to do the work and face the dangers of creating a farm from wilderness. He'd found it in Colorado, filed on it, built a cabin and barn, then headed back to Kansas to fetch his bride.

Laurie's parents were right. Caleb did have a good head on his shoulders, and he had chosen his young wife carefully. He knew exactly what stock Laurie came from, had watched her grow up. A good girl, she'd been raised to be proficient in a good farmwife's duties – cooking, cleaning, doing those things a woman did to keep a household running smoothly. She had a nice figure, too, and had never been sickly, so should have no trouble bearing his children.

It didn't hurt that she was pretty as well, and with a lively sense of humor. Also, he loved her; perhaps not the 'in love' of a young girl's dreams, though knowing her well, he'd never say such a thing to his new wife, but he loved her just the same.

Yet Laurie's strongest trait, as far as Caleb was concerned and after due consideration of Chitting's eligible female population, was her willingness to leave the life she'd always known and go with him. When he'd talked of finding farm-land in the frontier west, she'd not only been enthusiastic, she'd been all for it.

The young man was sublimely unaware that Laurie, too, had been pragmatic in her choice of spouse. Her new hand-some husband … and he *was* handsome … had decided they needed to make their life in the West, to her the possible adventure of a lifetime, and she had no hesitation in agreeing. With her very soul yearning for something different, he'd just provided her dearest wish.

While up till now, her travels might have been limited, Laurie was a reader, and her favorite books were those by or about women explorers; women who dared the unknown wilds of the earth, women who'd seen what no other white women had seen, done things few other white women had done. More than anything, Laurie wanted to be one of those fearless women. She'd read the diaries, heard the tales of young females like herself who braved the unknown, who went to distant lands where few women dared to venture.

For years she'd dreamed of joining the ranks of these intrepid souls, and now her new husband was taking her West to settle on the frontier of the relatively new state of Colorado – as exotic in Laurie's mind as darkest Africa.

Inhabited by savages and dangerous wild animals, this exotic land was right on Kansas's doorstep, and Caleb was willing to take her there.

Maybe someday her own diaries and letters home would be published, she thought, and she, too, would speak of her adventures at lecture halls and Chatauquas to enthrall the poor souls stuck in their mundane lives.

The way West would mean a long journey clear across Kansas and then onward over unknown land. Well, perhaps not *quite* unknown. Caleb had told her that part of their journey would be over the Santa Fe Trail, a fact thrilling Laurie even more. Her heroine, Susan Magoffin, had been the first white woman to travel that trail and now she, Laurie Cosgrove, would sit high and proud on their wagon seat just like Susan had almost fifty years ago – give or take.

It would be a hard life once they got where they were going, Caleb warned her, but Laurie saw herself standing stalwart at her husband's side through whatever dangers this move might bring. In Colorado, they would till soil that had never known a plow, and together they would bring civilization to an untamed land.

If she had to live without the modern conveniences, so what. She didn't care a snap and could hardly wait.

As the young couple set out, Laurie reminded her family to be sure and save the letters she would send them. They would be of historical significance someday, she promised.

Actually, they could have ridden the train most of the way and made better time, but Caleb was taking farm implements and Laurie had trunks of household goods and a few pieces of furniture, so they were going by wagon. Once they arrived at their homestead, they would need the mules pulling the wagon, too. Better to buy the animals in Kansas than in Colorado where such things were horribly expensive.

For several weeks, they traveled settled lands, the communities they passed through much like the one left behind, the roads well-traveled in both directions by farmers and freighters and passenger conveyances; generally, just people going about their usual business.

Laurie chafed, but faithfully mailed a letter home every chance she got describing their trip. With the scenery nothing she'd not seen before, in desperation she took to describing anything out of the ordinary they happened to come across. An oddly painted sign, a horse with ribbons tied in its mane, a woman's interesting bonnet. That sort of thing.

But, "That fellow didn't have a beard down to his knees," Caleb commented once, reading over her shoulder. "It only came to the middle of his chest. And it wasn't bright red."

"Maybe not, but it was sort of reddish and quite long," Laurie told him. "I'm sure in another couple of months it *will* be down to his knees. It's what we writers call creative license."

As they continued west, farms gave way to open grassland. Miles and miles of it as far as the eye could see, she wrote, the grass waving and undulating in the wind like a vast ocean. That was true. But sledges traveling over these grasslands? Not inconceivable, she reasoned, and so described those sledges in her next letter, mentioning the people riding in them who waved as they passed by.

And as she thought of a few of the descriptions she'd read in Annette Meakin's rail trip across the steppes of Russia, she wrote that the sledges were brightly painted with scrolls and birds and stylized flowers.

They were now on *the* famous Santa Fe Trail, to Laurie's delight, and the way was getting rougher, often the ruts cut so deep Caleb had to take the wagon far off to the side of them to make easier going. For her eager readers, and she was sure they were eager, she described the Arkansas River they now traveled beside and the 'new' fort William Bent had built after fire destroyed his 'old' one – the one Susan Magoffin, had been the first white woman to step inside.

Caleb stopped long enough for her to gaze over its remaining weed-choked rubble and allowed Laurie time enough to imagine what it would have been like had *she* been that first white woman. Alas, there were many white women living in the western lands now, so Laurie's time for being the first for anything stood little chance. Still, much of the West remained as frontier, she reminded herself, and she and Caleb could be called pioneers in their own right.

When mountains appeared on the far horizon, the sight of them, hazy as they were in the distance, excited Laurie so much that she bounced on the hard wagon seat and gave Caleb a little hug. For the first time in her life she was seeing real, honest-to-goodness mountains. At last, truly something *different* to write about.

A little danger wouldn't hurt, either, she thought regretfully. So far, in her opinion, the letters she sent home were just plain boring, no matter how hard she tried to liven them up.

The only wild animals they'd seen that were unknown to the people of Chittings were a few antelope and a small group of buffalo. The five buffalo were feeding quietly off in the distance, unbothered by their wagon's passing, but in Laurie's letter, those few buffalo became a stampeding herd with Caleb having to send the mules galloping over the prairie, the wagon careening over the uneven ground and almost throwing them out of it as they raced for their lives.

Well, it *could* have happened had the buffalo got riled up and taken a notion.

As for the day they'd seen the antelope, the animals had leaped away as the wagon approached, bounding out of sight so fast that Laurie couldn't get a good look at them. Her description of their grace and speed was powerfully vivid, nevertheless.

But now ... *mountains!* And the closer they got to them, the more there was to describe, for they were constantly changing, she told her readers quite truthfully ... their colors and contours shifting with the time of day, with the weather, with cloud shadow, even with the squint of an eye. Laurie's fingers ached, she wrote so much, trying to get the description just right for her readers at home. She needed no hyperbole now; the mountains were hyperbole in and of themselves.

When Caleb told her they would not be going as far as the mountain range itself, she was sorely disappointed. The land he'd filed on was in the foothills, he said. And it wouldn't be long now before they got there.

Seeing his wife's disappointment, Caleb tried to soften the blow by describing, with some hesitation, the cabin he'd built for her. In the beginning, with Laurie's excitement over the journey itself, somehow he'd never got around to mentioning the cabin awaiting them at the end of it. It had only one room for now, he said diffidently. Made of logs from trees he'd cut and shaped himself, it wouldn't be pretty, he warned. And it ... well, it had a dirt floor. Also, there was a rancher nearby who might not be ... Caleb coughed ... friendly.

A log cabin that her husband had made himself, and with a dirt floor? To Caleb's surprise, Laurie perked up immediately and sent him a dazzling smile.

Oh, my goodness. How perfectly wonderful. Not for this rugged pioneer couple a white two-story farmhouse like the ones they'd both come from. Oh, no. They were settling a new land so of course the living arrangements would be barely adequate.

There would be so much to write about.

THEIR LAND WAS five miles outside the community of Harding but, needing to pick up foodstuffs and supplies before settling in, they stopped in town first before going on to the cabin. To Laurie's delight, Harding, Colorado wasn't at all like Chittings, Kansas. For one thing, it was a town not fifteen years old and still rough around the edges. She and Caleb weren't the only ones carving out new lives for themselves.

Freight wagons, buckboards, and buggies of every sort crowded Harding's busy dust-filled main street. On the walkways, Laurie saw farmers and business owners looking much the same as those in any small town in Kansas, but she also saw cowboys and prospectors and miners, native Indians, Chinese, and Mexicans, even a man wearing a turban. She heard languages she'd never heard before that sounded wonderfully different -- musical or guttural, but definitely exotic. Even some of the English sounded different.

With no time to savor this banquet of newness, however, she squirreled the sights and sounds and smells away in her memory to write about as soon as she had time. Right now, she needed to spend Caleb's carefully hoarded coins for fresh supplies to set up housekeeping.

Laurie found the general store just as much a wonderland of colors and scents as the street outside its screen door. With its treasure trove of items for uses she could only guess at she longed to pelt the busy man behind the counter with questions. The place was full of customers, however, with no one standing idly about talking as they would have been back home. Another time, then. She paid for her purchases and, since one corner of the store served as a post office, mailed the several letters she'd been accumulating.

Caleb needn't have worried. When he turned off the main road onto their land, Laurie was immediately enchanted. A sweeping meadow, forest in the distance. Hovering over all, jagged snowcapped mountains. To Laurie's mind, the small cabin and barn completed a picture as beautiful as any painting. Nor was she disappointed at the cabin's sparse interior … not its dirt floor nor its fireplace made of river rock. A mansion couldn't have made her happier. Even as she gazed around, words flew around her mind like so many twittering birds, detailing the inadequacies of her new home that pleased her right down to the ground.

THE NEXT DAY, with Caleb somewhere out on the property,

Laurie was in the cabin trying, without much success, to organize their food supplies when three riders approached the cabin.

Visitors! How nice. She patted her hair and hurried out to greet them.

The three looked grim and forbidding, but Laurie didn't notice their expressions. She was too busy raptly gazing at their trappings and thrilling to what she saw.

Real cowboys! Wait till she told the family.

Smiling widely, she called out a delighted, "Hello," before any of them could speak. "Are you our neighbors? Caleb said there was a ranch nearby. I've never seen real cowboys before. Why, you're absolutely splendid." And she clasped her hands to her breast and beamed up at them.

"Ma'am …" the one in the middle began, his tone rough.

"Oh, no," she interrupted. "Don't call me ma'am. I'm Laurie Cosgrove. My husband is Caleb Cosgrove. We just arrived yesterday and are so excited to be in this breath-taking land. We just love it already!"

"Well, that's the thing, Ma'am. You can't …."

"And you are…?" she asked, her face bright and smiling.

"Paul Hanover," he clipped out. "Ma'am, is your husband…."

"Laurie," she said. "Not *Ma'am*. After all, we're neighbors."

"About that…." Hanover tried again.

"Oh, where are my manners? Won't you get down from your horses and come in? You will be my first guests. And I'm dying to ask about your hats."

The men looked at each other. "Our hats?" one of them asked.

"I'm sorry. Am I being rude? I don't know western ways yet. It's just that I've heard so much about them. Please come in and have a cup of coffee so we can get acquainted. You can tell me all about what it's like to live in this wonderful place. I'm sure Caleb will come when he sees we have company."

The men looked at each other again. "Ma'am...."

When they hesitated, "Please," she said ... pleaded actually. She thought she might cry, wanting so much to get a good look at these cowboys she'd only read about in books and seen on posters advertising wild west shows.

Looking vaguely uncomfortable, the men swung down from their horses.

In the cabin they ranged themselves around the small table, the cowboys examining the rough interior with a bureau and bedstead looking out of place on the dirt floor and sacks and boxes scattered around that needed a place to go. Laurie bustled about pouring coffee.

"Are these your sons?" she asked Mr. Hanover, smiling at the two younger men.

"Er, no. These are my hands, Roy and Tucker."

Laurie dipped a shy little curtsy. "I'm happy to meet you," she said. "Are you real buckaroos?"

Both men turned beet red.

"Back home, everybody's favorite reading is about real western buckaroos," Laurie confided. "Wild Bill Hickock and Buffalo Bill and Annie Oakley. They call her Little Miss Sureshot, you know. Have you met her? I always wished I could see one of their wild west shows, but they never came to our part of Kansas. But Caleb and I are doing something so much better, don't you think? Instead of just watching, we're actually *living* in this wonderful place, just like you are."

She took a breath to add admiringly, "I see you're wearing guns. Caleb knows how to shoot, but I want to learn, too. Maybe someday I'll be as good as Little Miss Sureshot."

The younger cowboy gave a small cough.

Before any of them quite knew how it happened, the men at the table set about describing their lives for her, in the process throwing a few sly digs at each other, too. When Laurie said she thought Caleb should get a pair of boots like they wore, Paul Hanover told her gravely they might not be the best footwear for a farmer.

It took a while for Laurie to realize the men didn't like her coffee, a realization that set her to blushing and apologizing. "I don't quite have the hang of cooking in a fireplace," she said, "and Caleb doesn't know how, either. Our folks had iron stoves back home." She confessed it as if embarrassed by such excess on their two families' part.

"Don't you worry about it, Ma'am ... uh, Laurie. Your coffee just seems a little tame to us, uh, buckaroos, that's all. We usually drink ours horseshoe strong." He sent a covert wink to his cowhands. "And my wife has an iron stove she's quite proud of. I doubt she knows how to cook in a fireplace, either, but I do. Used to do it in the cabin I had when I first arrived in these parts. Let me give you a few pointers."

Much to his hands surprise, he squatted in front of the fireplace and showed Laurie a few tricks for better cooking. She squatted beside him, spellbound, gazing at him with awe. "Wait till I write to them back home how good you are at this. Why, such things are truly a lost art," she told him seriously.

Hanover's chest puffed out a bit. He went on to give her a few pointers on how to store and keep critters out of her foodstuffs, too.

As they emerged from the cabin into the bright morning sunlight to be on their way a few minutes later, Caleb came running toward the cabin, looking scared but determined. He carried a rifle.

As a group, the men stiffened, but Laurie called out, "Oh, Caleb, look who's come to visit us. This is our neighbor, Mr. Hanover, and these are his hands, Roy and Tucker. They're real cowboys. And do you know, Mr. Hanover once met Wild Bill Hickock. Isn't that amazing?"

Caleb came to a halt, standing just in front of Laurie. "Hanover," he said shortly, with a nod equally as short.

But Paul Hanover stuck out his hand. "Glad to meet you, Cosgrove. Laurie here's told us all about you. Fine girl. I'm sure the wife would like to meet her. Come see us sometime. As your missus says, this is a big wide *breathtakin'* land, so I reckon there's room enough for a farmer and a rancher if we both keep our work to our own side of the fence. The times are changin', I guess. You just build your fences tight like I'll be buildin' mine. Wouldn't want my cattle messin' up your wheat fields or your wheat fields siphonin' off water from my grass."

"Don't reckon I'd want that, either," Caleb said. "And I'm a good fence builder." He shook Hanover's hand.

That night after supper, by lantern light and while sitting at the table that wobbled a bit on the uneven ground, Laurie wrote to the family back home about the buckaroos who'd come to visit, telling her parents and siblings how cowboys liked their coffee so strong a horseshoe could float in it and that *real* cowboys had explained to her that easterners (written with some derision) had got it all wrong. A *real* (heavily underlined) cowboy's hat didn't hold ten gallons but only one. Much of what had been written about cowboys was purely exaggeration, she explained.

On Sunday, Laurie made another discovery. She and Caleb went into town to see if there was a church they could attend. There was, a white nondescript building with a bell steeple. It did double duty as schoolhouse and meeting hall for dances and political harangues when not in use as a church. And it was non-denominational, one of the parishioners explained. Laurie hadn't known you could worship in a church that was non-denominational and not go straight to

Hell, but the preacher wasted no time calling down fire and brimstone just like the preacher did at home, and the congregation seemed friendly and no more hell-bound than those in the First Baptist church in Chittings. When she wrote about the experience, however, she worded her letter carefully, mentioning no specific denomination. She didn't want her parents to worry.

The next time Laurie and Caleb went into town, they found letters from home waiting for them, the first they'd had since starting their journey. And Laurie had one that sent her into transports so strong that she uttered a small scream right on the porch in front of the general store. Too excited to stand still, she gave herself a little half twirl, then grinned at everyone who'd stopped to gape. "They're printing my letters in the *Chittings Gazette*," she told the elderly couple staring at her.

"That's nice, dear," the woman replied, and hurried her husband on down the walkway.

From that day on, knowing her audience had grown to far more than just her family, Laurie's letter writing became a crusade. She wrote often and vividly, adjectives and adverbs fluttering through her prose like so much colorful confetti. When she further learned her adventurous accounts were being picked up by other area newspapers in Kansas, too, she thought life just couldn't get better.

Though written in letter form, she had her own column circulating throughout the state and headlined *Life in the Wild West with Mrs. Laura Cosgrove,* her mother wrote to her. She was famous.

Nor was she ever short of material to write about. For Laurie, there was little about her life that wasn't glorious adventure. Just ask Caleb or her friends and neighbors.

When hailstones big as baseballs flattened their first crop and sent Caleb running out to get the mules and their cow into the barn before they were beaten to death, she wrote about it in glorious detail. Yes, they had hailstorms sometimes in Kansas, but this storm was bigger and far more dangerous. Beside her at the table where she was writing, Caleb too sat with pencil and paper, only he was trying to figure out if they could make it financially through the coming year.

Laurie wasn't worried. The paper was paying her a penny a word by this time, and she had plenty of words.

There was the rattlesnake she found curled up on the step when she opened the cabin door one morning. It was ten feet long and had two dozen rattles. All right, so maybe only four feet with perhaps half a dozen rattles, but Laurie knew her readers wouldn't want the story to be *dull*. So while she wasn't the one to actually kill it – Caleb did – she was, after all, the one who saw it first and warned her husband of the danger.

When Caleb gave her the rattles, she pinned them to the buckaroo hat she wore for work in her vegetable garden or when she helped Caleb in the fields.

She'd been practicing with Caleb's rifle, too, and when a panther came prowling around the corral one early evening when Caleb was still in the fields, she shot it. Well, she shot *at* it and it ran away. In a moment of candor, she told her faithful readers that while she wasn't Little Miss Sureshot yet, she was working on it.

The arrowheads she found on the property … or the *artifacts*, as they should be called, had Laurie envisioning herself as a modern time Hester Stanhope. She even donned a pair of Caleb's britches as she began searching for more 'artifacts' turned up by her husband's plow. However, Caleb didn't care at all about Hester Stanhope's archaeological digs in the Holy Land and threw such a fit when he saw his wife in trousers that Laurie was forced to go back to her usual skirts – an incident not mentioned in her letters, by the way.

A year and more went by. Laurie was pregnant, but she was doing fine, she told her mother. Mrs. Hanover, who had become a good friend and who had a daughter close to Laurie's age, checked on and clucked over her regularly, and the ladies at church offered plenty of advice. It was all wonderful. A new life for a new land.

Until it wasn't. Laurie's letter writing stopped abruptly, and it was Caleb who notified her parents and his that she had lost their baby. Her body had easily recovered from the loss, he told them, but his wife's spirits didn't. He was worried.

When another month went by with still no letters, Laurie's mother suggested to Caleb that he send her back to Kansas for a spell.

A daughter her parents had never encountered before arrived at the train station, looking wan and listless, and seemingly interested in not much of anything.

They worried … until, that is, after a couple of weeks of painful conversations answered with monosyllables and coupled with picky eating and too many naps, in a moment of inspiration, her mother casually passed to her daughter the weekly *Chittings Gazette*.

Without much interest, Laurie dutifully scanned the headlines and, with a heavy sigh, turned the page for features of local interest … recipes and such.

"Oh," she said, sitting up straight on the couch where'd she'd been half reclined, her gaze now fixed on the column headed *Life in the Wild West with Mrs. Laura Cosgrove.* For the first time she saw her writing in print.

Well.

Just … well.

But she hadn't written anything for the last few months. How was it the paper was still featuring her accounts?

Her mother explained. As prolific as she was, Laurie had been sending home three or four letters a week, but the weekly paper only featured one at a time. There was a backlog.

And, by the way, the president of the Women's Literary Society of Chittings had asked if Laurie would like to be the featured speaker at their next meeting.

Laurie would love to. Fulfilled at last was her dream of being a famous female explorer, with her adventures not only in print but the public wanting to hear the details for themselves.

As it turned out, however, part of that dream was not to be. Chatauquas and lecture halls would have to do without her.

Standing in front of the Women's Literary Society of Chittings, her knees quaking, her stomach roiling, her notes trembling in her hand, the usually intrepid Laurie came to the realization that she was much better at writing than she was at making speeches. She did her best that warm afternoon but vowed that from now on she would stick to what she did best. Speaking engagements just weren't for her. Her fame must rest solely on her writing.

She also took a good look around and saw that her hometown hadn't changed a bit from the time she'd left it almost three years ago. She missed the mountains; she missed the excitement of not knowing what the day would bring when she awoke each morning. She missed Caleb. In Kansas, there was nothing to write that everyone didn't already know, but in the West there were new adventures around every corner. Besides, the *Chittings Gazette* would run out of her letters soon. She wanted to go home and write more.

Her parents put Laurie on the train, her mother teary, her

father resigned, both glad for their daughter's returned health, and both doing admirable jobs at hiding their relief at her readiness to return to points West. As with everything their eldest daughter did ... with the exception of public speaking ... Laurie did 'wan and listless' extremely well. And, they told themselves, judging by her correspondence, she could handle anything thrown at her by that wild untamed country she loved so much.

Perhaps not the loss of a child, but no woman anywhere could handle that well.

Caleb was glad to have his wife back. She brought a glamor to his life that personally he couldn't see but she could, and he was happy to believe her.

Over the years, the farm prospered, and Laurie gave birth to three more children – two boys and a girl – with no trouble this time, recognized or ignored. Always, she wrote home describing her life in extravagant detail, its greatest dangers, its greatest joys, its uniqueness in every way.

Because she herself found excitement in all things different, it took Laurie a while to see that the West was no longer as unique to the world as it once had been. She and Caleb had been at the tail end of the pioneers, those coming after them migrating to the land of opportunity as investors and business owners rather than to tame it themselves. With towns springing up everywhere, railroads now made swift and easy connections that only a few years ago would have been impossible.

Laurie's column bit the dust, never to be resurrected.

The affairs of the world were encroaching, as well. Taking centerstage in the newspapers, both national and local, the sinking of the *Maine* and the resulting mayhem afterward became the focus of the country's attention. Just a few years after that, European affairs just couldn't seem to stay in Europe.

Laurie continued to write letters home, however. After all, life in the West was still exciting. The West never did completely settle down to the level of the staid East. Cowpokes still wore their boots and their ten gallon hats that didn't hold ten gallons. Laurie herself still wore her own ten gallon hat with the rattlesnake's calling card attached to it. But the log cabin Caleb built for her had long since been torn down to make way for a white, two-story, four-bedroom farmhouse much like the ones they'd both grown up in and where she now cooked on a modern state-of-the art stove. Gas lighting lit the homes in Harding, with some saying electricity would be the energy of the future.

The Cosgrove and Hanover fences might have been built strong, but not so strong that the eldest Cosgrove boy and the eldest Hanover granddaughter were kept from marrying. That's how, ultimately, the fences between the properties came down and the C-H ranch became one of the largest in that part of Colorado. Laurie's youngest boy went to law school and returned to practice in Harding. He married well and later became a judge. But his sister … like mother like daughter, always looking for adventure, Laurie's friends said with fond smiles … ran off with a cowboy from Texas, a state older than the state of Colorado but still wearing its rough heritage like a badge of honor. They settled on a ranch in Far West Texas, an area as near to actual frontier as one could get.

With every day still a day of adventure for her, through it all Laurie continued to write.

She died at forty-six from a rattlesnake bite.

Maybe that old tattered cowboy hat she never gave up wearing was bad luck, some thought, but Laurie probably would have chosen this kind of death over one that had her old, feeble, and bedridden. It made for better copy. The whole town and surrounding countryside turned out for the funeral, the event rating a full column in the *Harding Caller Times,* with the writer sparing neither fulsome adjectives nor scintillating adverbs. Laurie would have been delighted.

In 1955, one of Laura Cosgrove's great nephews found her letters and corresponding newspaper clippings in a box tied up with faded green ribbon in his great great grandmother's attic in Kansas. Curious, he began to read ... and his eyes widened at the historical value he was sure these letters contained. He published them in book form at his own expense, giving the volume the same title the *Chittings Gazette* had bestowed on the column so long ago: *Life in the Wild West with Mrs. Laura Cosgrove.*

To his disappointment, history scholars didn't snatch the volume up as a newly discovered primary historical source but dismissed it with scholarly disdain. It contained far too many exaggerations and distorted known facts for them to take it seriously, they said. It did, however, provide a few dry chuckles over glasses of Scotch. One likened it to the Disney version of Davy Crockett.

However, Laurie could have told them they got a few things wrong themselves.

Her story about having her second child while alone in the cabin during a horrendous thunderstorm with lightning bouncing all around? Probably true, the scholars said. The dates were correct for a storm known in the annals of bad weather phenomena.

Well, that one *wasn't* quite true. Caleb was with her.

Her account of chasing a bear out of the cabin with a broom?

They poo-pooed the account, but it had happened just as Laurie wrote it.

One thing the scholars agreed on, though. They loved the enthusiasm and joie de vivre with which the woman wrote. If one didn't take it seriously, it was a delightful read.

Thus, for several years the few volumes of the nephew's book still in existence sat in dusty obscurity on library and used bookstore shelves. Recently, however, for dealers in such things, it's beginning to gain a bit of value as a rare but certainly not definitive work, though finding it at a tag sale or charity shop will never make anyone's fortune.

For Laurie, however, just knowing her writing is still available to the reading public would probably be fortune enough.

A SOCIETY OF WIDOWS

The widder eats by a bell; she gits up by a bell – everything's so awful reg'lar a body can't stand it.

Mark Twain
The Adventures of Tom Sawyer (1876)

A SOCIETY OF WIDOWS

I MIGHT AS WELL BE IN THAT BOX WITH YOU.

Though Emma stood at her late husband's graveside, her thought was not one of sorrow. She and George had never really loved each other.

Oh, for goodness sake, woman! You're being maudlin and looking for something to blame your dismals on. Of course you loved George.

They'd just never been 'in love,' that's all. Lusted a little for one another, perhaps. She'd been a pretty girl and George Williams a handsome up-and-coming young man. And, they'd rubbed along nicely together, comfortable with the thought of what each had to offer in a marriage. She, finding his ambition an asset to future stability; he, finding her womanly skills and social abilities an asset to his rising fortunes. So they'd married.

And it was a good marriage. Don't forget that.

As young marrieds they'd come west where George, with a loan from his father, set up a hauling business in the small settlement of Myers Ferry. A ramshackle ferry business and a few equally ramshackle buildings at the easiest crossing of the Azuleja River were the town's only reason for existence. If you could call it a town back then.

When George and Emma arrived, however, George had seen the makeshift settlement's potential, and he'd been right. He'd filed on land and established his hauling business to take advantage of the existing ferry. In addition, wise in the way of commerce, George invested in the various enterprises the opening of the west gave rise to. Myers Ferry prospered, and the growing Williams family prospered with it. What had once been ramshackle became a small stable community, then a larger one.

Yet a little over a year ago, George had not been wise when he decided to take the first ferry of the day across the river and travel to a nearby town to investigate possible investments there. What's more, he'd taken their oldest son Georgie with him. Georgie was delighted to go, proud that now he was twenty-two his father had decided he was mature enough for partnership and was grooming him accordingly.

After breakfast that fateful morning, both father and son gave Emma a hasty peck on the cheek in farewell and said they'd return the following day. There had been a storm the night before, but the morning sun shone bright and clear with promise of a lovely day.

As usual, the Azuleja had flooded during the storm, but the river had crested and the water was back in its banks by the time the sun rose, also a usual occurrence in this thirsty country. It still ran high, however, but had dropped low enough the ferryman apparently had no qualms about making an early morning run. His had not been a wise decision, either. Halfway across the river, he hadn't seen the submerged clump of tree branches until there was no way to avoid it. All aboard perished ... George and Georgie, the ferryman, and a family of three going home after visiting relatives.

Emma had grieved when George died. Had grieved for him and her son, grieved for their healthy and vigorous lives cut short. But now, a year later, standing alone at their gravesides on this warm summer day, her grief was for herself, for *her* loss of a healthy and vigorous life.

Yes, she was still healthy and still vigorous, but her life wasn't.

With a quiet sigh, Emma placed one of three bouquets of flowers from her garden into the urn affixed to George's marker, lay another on Georgie's grave, and the last on that of her daughter Judith who ten years ago had died of influenza. Most of her family lay at her feet now. But not all. Miles east, twenty-year-old Patrick, her only remaining child, worked for the railroad as it built its way westward. For all intents and purposes, she was now alone.

With that in mind, she'd briefly considered returning to Illinois where she'd grown up, but her parents had been dead for years and her only sister now lived in Ohio. The sisters' letters were sporadic at best, any closeness they'd once shared now a thing of the past. Emma decided to remain in Myers Ferry where she had enough money to see her into a comfortable old age. Her home was free and clear and one of the nicest in town. As a member of one of the community's first families, she enjoyed a certain social prestige, as well. Just as important, she had friends here,

So I thought. Where are those friends now?

Having always been civic minded and an organizer, the growing community of Myers Ferry was fertile ground for a woman of Emma's talents. She'd been a leading instigator in getting a school built. She was the one who had written the letter of request to church fathers back in the States for a pastor to serve the Myers Ferry faithful, promising to see to it a church was built for him should he come. Which he did, and she did. Over the years, she'd served on countless civic committees as the town's status changed from a here-today-gone-tomorrow frontier settlement to a stable community with a mayor and named streets. One of those named streets was Williams Street on which her home was located.

All meaning diddly-squat!

All right, she was brooding. She knew it. She, who never brooded.

But, looking back, the change had been so gradual. Gradual to the point that only recently had she fully realized there *was* a change. Oh, she'd known she was growing increasingly lonely but blamed it on adjusting to the loss of her husband and oldest son and the kind of silences her home had never known before.

The day of George and Georgie's drowning was still a blur. All she really remembered of it was being surrounded by people, women from the church and her various women's groups mostly, who had come to be with her, to sit with her in her darkened parlor. She remembered endless hands patting hers, people talking to her but not seeming to mind when she didn't answer. Someone made coffee and served it, she didn't know who. Another unknown someone contributed tea cakes and saw to it they were passed around.

The whole first week following the funerals there'd been a constant stream of visitors, many of the women taking over the necessary chores to keep a household in mourning func-tioning, most of them bringing food, far too much of it for her and Patrick to eat. She sent most of it home with Imelda, her cook and housekeeper, who came every day even with little to do but wash their few dishes.

That was the first week. The second week saw fewer visi-tors, and those only stayed for a short while. None brought covered dishes. In Illinois, such guests would not have visited personally but would simply leave cards acknowledging her bereavement. In the West, however, things were more face to face, and grief a short-lived luxury. Western life demanded it be got on with, and quickly. And by that second week, that's exactly what Emma needed for herself; to again take up the hostess reins with these visitors, pouring the coffee, passing 'round Imelda's small desserts, filling any conversational gaps that might occur. In short, doing what she did best again, a normalcy her sorrow craved. A normalcy she planned to continue.

Patrick returned to his job with the railroad that week, a job having something to do with surveying, she thought, but wasn't sure. Unlike his brother, he'd never shown interest in his father's various businesses and encouraged Emma to sell them if she did not want to manage them herself. She didn't. She knew little about business. What she knew about was running her home, running a church bazaar, organizing box suppers to benefit whomever or whatever needed a money boost, and overseeing her community's moral and cultural needs. So she followed Patrick's advice and sold George's holdings, setting aside half the money for Patrick's inheritance and knowing the other half would keep herself solvent for life.

She remained on the various committees she was a part of following George's death, and continued her participation with several women's groups, most of which she'd founded. Her days remained full.

The evenings….

Well.

Evenings used to be the time when one could breathe a peaceful sigh and call it a day. It had been a time for family conversations and updates around the dining room table. Afterward, she and George sat in the parlor, George reading the newspaper, she with a book or doing whatever fancy work or mending that was in her workbasket. A peaceful time.

Now she was drowning in that peace, and there was little she could do about it. As a lone woman she couldn't go out of an evening unless she was invited. These days, she was seldom invited.

To escape the overwhelming silence at the dining room table, now she often ate her supper at the kitchen table now, chatting with Imelda as her housekeeper went about clearing up.

There was no Imelda to sit with in the parlor after supper, though. Emma sat alone.

And there was no one but Emma in that big bed upstairs, either. That's where she truly missed George. Their joinings had been seldom these past years, either George was uninterested, or she was, or they both were. But she missed his large warm body lying next to hers, his back often a bulwark to her own, missed his rumbling snores that had been background to her sleep throughout all her married life. Now the very silence of the bedroom kept her awake.

Squatting, Emma rubbed the fingers of one hand over George's name on the headstone. GEORGE WHITTINGTON WILLIAMS. There was a space on the stone for her own name when the time came. Her lips quirked slightly, the smile rueful. 'Emma Jane Langston Williams' would not look nearly as imposing George's name did. The plot beside his waited for her occupancy, too. Standing abruptly, Emma glared at that empty plot.

I'm not ready for it yet, George!

So why did she feel she was being pushed into it? Her lonely evenings were only to be expected, but wasn't she living her life much as she had before George's death? Yet lately, as she went about her committee work and attended various meetings, she often felt as if she'd not only lost

George and Georgie, but something else. Something vital. But what?

The answer reached out and slapped into her brain with such force she caught her breath. *Because I've lost who I am. I don't know me anymore.*

That's why, moments ago, she'd allowed herself to think she should be in the grave with George. Because, without him, who was she?

Oh, good lord, Emma Jane Langston Williams. You know exactly who you are. It's the good people of Myers Ferry who can't figure out what to do with you if you're not running a meeting of some kind.

Snatching up a long weed stem that shouldn't be there – Emma organized a cemetery clean-up every year – she began pacing the neat paths between the plots, absently swishing a tombstone now and then with the weed's feathery head as she reviewed her current life with new awareness.

It was at church where she should have had the first inklings that things were changing for her, though she hadn't paid attention to it then. The fact that she no longer had family to sit beside in church was obvious, but following the service, when people usually stood around outside the church doors and chatted awhile, she found she had no one to chat with. Couples with whom she and George had been friends would stop and greet her but soon moved on to talk more extensively with other couples. Emma was no longer part of a couple.

Come to think of it, talk of interest to women only happened during the day when their men were at work. But with women of Emma's age, it was *couples* talk after church.

Odd she'd never noticed that before, probably because she and George had a busy social life. They'd frequently entertained friends and business acquaintances in their home and been entertained as frequently in the homes of others. On Imelda's days off, they'd often gone to the restaurant in the hotel for lunch or dinner, something Emma hadn't done since George died. Not only was dining alone in a public setting socially unacceptable for a woman, it would be downright embarrassing.

Her social life now? Nil. Witness those lonely evenings at home.

On occasion she was still invited to friends' homes for dinner, but those invitations had grown fewer over time. And, if she was honest, often seemed reluctantly given. More a token invitation for an important committee member, she suspected, than a true wish for her presence. She was a lone woman invited to dinner in a *couple's* home, where it seemed if she laughed at a witticism thrown out by the husband of the house or joined too heartily in a topic of conversation, his wife, with whom she thought she'd been friends for years, would grow progressively more silent and send her repressive looks.

Good heavens, did these women think she was *flirting* with their husbands on these occasions? But why? She never behaved in any way she hadn't behaved countless times before when George was alive. But then, with her husband beside her, she too had been part of a couple. With a husband beside her, her laughter was no more than good humor, her engaged conversation no more than what was expected of her. She could be who she was … *with her husband beside her.* But as a widow, if there were married men around, she was supposed to blend into the woodwork.

Well … well, *damn!*

And unmarried men? If she wanted to marry again, there was no shortage of them ready to take on the role of husband. George was hardly cold in his grave before many of the town bachelors came calling. Men with an eye toward a rich widow, she'd bet. Why such men needed her money when they seemed more than capable of earning it the same way George had, she couldn't fathom.

Then there were the widowers, young and old. Younger men left with children still at home after their wives died. However much they might talk pretty, there was little romance involved and no one pretended otherwise. What these men were looking for was a mother for their children and someone to cook for them and keep their homes – or move themselves and their family into Emma's home. But she didn't want to raise another family. She'd already raised one, with all the attendant joys, sorrows, trials and tribulations it entailed. She didn't want to raise another. Someday Patrick would marry and give her grandchildren. That was enough.

Older widowers? No romance there, either. They wanted a live-in housekeeper-companion.

Well there is that, I suppose. The way things are looking, it might not be such a bad idea.

But really, did she want to marry again? Emma wasn't sure. Other than the lonely nights, there was a certain freedom in no longer having to answer to a man or have the need to fit her life around his.

Still, such freedom definitely had its drawbacks. As a widow she was now subject to the kind of gossip and conjecture she'd never dreamed would someday be leveled at herself. She saw eyebrows raised if on the street she so much as said good morning to a single man, or exchanged a word or two with a married one as she browsed the goods in the mercantile. She knew exactly what that kind of gossip was like, for hadn't she been guilty of it herself where other widows were concerned when she, too, had been securely part of a couple?

That word again.

Any interaction with a man at all had a widow labeled as

man-hungry. Nor was it just the women doing the labeling. Many men, too, made such an assumption. She'd already been on the receiving end of remarks that never would have been uttered if George were alive.

Things might have been easier had she decided to return to Illinois, to Chicago perhaps. There, much of society's expectations for women had more to do with financial status than with marital status. As a wealthy woman, she could eat alone in one of the city's many restaurants and no one would bat an eye. Her fashion sense might be the subject of avid gossip but not the fact she said good morning to a man on the street. An exaggeration, perhaps, but not much of one.

In the west, however, financial status didn't mean as much. Men, rich or poor, were judged on how well they could be counted on in a crisis and whether or not their word was good. Women, on the other hand, fell into only two categories. Rich or poor, she was either a 'good woman' or she was not.

Unless, that is, she was a widow. As Emma was learning, the community didn't seem to know how to label a widow, thus forcing such women into a grey area somewhere between 'good' and 'not.' She was a woman neither single nor wed, but she was … *knowledgeable.* Unmarried now, but no innocent. And a *knowledgeable* unmarried woman definitely had to tread carefully so as not to step over the 'good' and 'not' dividing line, a line frequently arbitrary and often invisible to the unwary.

Which is exactly what I've been doing these past months, treading on eggshells, afraid someone might think I'm a loose woman.

No wonder she felt out of touch with herself. How in the world did other widows cope with such nonsense? With always staying quiet and unobtrusive in public, becoming mere shadows of their true selves to appease suspicious minds?

Dropping the stem but still deep in thought, Emma turned to leave the cemetery, only to stop abruptly on the dusty path.

She wasn't the only widow in Myers Ferry. She knew of two in her quilting circle, and a few others she encountered who were forced to work during the day if their deceased husbands hadn't left them enough to live on. Menial jobs, usually. What other kinds were there for women with few skills?

She didn't know many of these women well, though she'd been friends with one or two back when they, too, had been part of a couple. Sad to say, she hadn't really noticed when those friendships faded away after the husband's passing, much like what she was finding now.

Starting on her way again, Emma's stride picked up speed. She must do something. She was tired of being viewed as something she was not. Life in the shadows was simply not for her.

How *did* other widows cope?

❧

THAT WEDNESDAY EVENING, six women sat down to supper at Emma's dining table. Their ages ranged from forties to around mid-sixties, and all were widows who'd led full lives while their husbands were alive but were now seemingly expected to have no lives at all outside of good works, church, and family, if they had one.

In planning the gathering, Emma decided that young widows, those with young children, had a right to be man-hungry, or ought to be. Probably their children were hungry, too. They *needed* a husband. Not one to give them a social life, but one to provide for life's basic needs. She'd never really considered their plight before, but come this winter, she planned to make certain the quilting circle remembered these young women. And at the next box supper, she would personally see to it their baskets went first to the most responsible of the eligible men. The other single girls could have the leftovers.

Tonight, however, was for those widows who, like herself, needed to somehow cope with their single status and get out of the shadow world being forced on them. Just because their husbands had met their maker and their children were grown or gone didn't mean they, too, should be boxed up and buried.

At first, conversation around the table lagged. With a couple of exceptions, none of the women knew each other well or had anything in common beyond their widowhood. Judging from Emma's own experience, most had probably responded to her invitation because they were so seldom invited out of an evening. Emma herself was hosting her first dinner party since George died, and her first dinner party ever that had not been exclusively for couples.

When the women at last wore out the topic of 'such a delicious pot roast' and 'my, what creamy mashed potatoes,' into the awkward lull Emma commented, "I'm tired of having to be so careful with everything I say to a man for fear someone will take it the wrong way."

There was a shocked silence. Finally, "Me, too," replied the shy Mrs. Banks, her voice barely above a whisper.

Emma added, "I swear, if I say so much as a 'how do you do' to somebody's husband, his wife takes offence."

"Why, you daring hussy, you," another threw out, her tone full of humorous but understanding sarcasm.

"Sometimes I wish I really was a hussy," another said with a sigh.

The group laughed, each of them knowing what the woman was really saying.

"Me, too," the shy Mrs. Banks murmured.

And they were off, the conversation lively now and often full of laughter as they complained and commiserated over the changes in their lifestyle as produced by their widowhood.

It continued over coffee taken in Emma's parlor, the topics sometimes serious, sometimes humorous, occasionally ribald. All of these women had been married and found they could say things to each other they could never speak of with their married friends and certainly not with their grown children. Some missed their husband's presence in their bed; some did not. Actually, some did not miss their husbands, either, but all missed former lives that now seemed denied them by the community.

The clock had chimed ten before the last woman left, the women thanking Emma for the enjoyable evening and hoping they could do it again.

It *had* been an enjoyable evening, Emma thought as she made her way upstairs to bed. In fact, it was the most enjoyable evening she'd spent since she'd lost George. Who knew a group of women could be so entertaining, or how liberating it could be to speak of things no one but another widow could understand. Finally having one's loneliness and angers acknowledged without judgement or condemnation had been as life-restoring as a dose of good medicine.

At this first gathering, a couple of the women had commented on how much they missed having a reason to dress up for an evening engagement. Such occasions happened so seldom these days, one mourned.

With such comments in mind, a couple of weeks later Emma organized an evening musicale, featuring those widows so inclined as the performers, but all of them invited as guests. The excited musicians rehearsed for days, chairs were set up in Emma's parlor, and family and friends were given invitations to attend. Two of the widows performed a classical piece on violin and viola with Emma accompanying them at the piano. Then a trio harmonized on music currently popular back in the States. As an encore, the shy Mrs. Banks led the audience in a sing-along. Every widow had dressed in her best for the small concert, some wearing colors other than black or gray and a few sporting nice pieces of jewelry. A good time, as they say, was had by all.

Next, it was an evening of enthusiastic parlor games, but for the widowed women only. After asking Emma's permission, one of them brought a couple of her own widow friends, so that little by little over the weeks, the gatherings grew larger.

Only on rare occasions was the public invited, and then only if the widows themselves agreed to it and did the inviting. In Emma's home, there would be no shadow persons.

And then one evening Patrick unexpectantly paid a visit home and brought his supervisor with him. Several widows were sitting around the dining table, lengthened now with both leaves, chattering and enjoying a potluck supper ('so nice to have someone to cook for besides myself') when Emma left the table to see who had just come into her home unannounced.

Patrick caught her up in a hug before introducing his companion. "This is Mr. Clyde Suderland, Mother. I told him you'd give us a homecooked meal, but I'm hearing guests. Should we leave?"

Her only remaining child. She couldn't turn him away. Everyone would just have to adjust, Patrick and friend to a roomful of women, and the widows to added guests ... *male* guests.

"So pleased to meet you, Mr. Suderland," she said, shaking

hands. "We're just a few friends having a potluck. You're welcome to join us, if you like."

Reasonably attractive. Clean. Mid to late fifties, perhaps. And from out of town. Where is the harm?

The men followed her into the dining room where the group at the table immediately fell silent. Emma introduced Mr. Suderland, placing faint emphasis on the fact that he was from out of town and in Myers Ferry with Patrick simply for a brief visit. "And a homecooked meal," she added, echoing Patrick's words with a smile.

Although clearly taken aback at finding only women present, Clyde Suderland rose to the occasion. "Ladies," he said, and gave a small courtly bow. Extra chairs were brought, those at the table scooting over to make room. Dishes were passed to the newcomers, but the animated chatter of moments before had died on the vine.

Mr. Suderland cleared his throat. "What creamy mashed potatoes," he said, breaking the silence.

Somebody giggled, another laughed outright.

"An inside joke, Mr. Suderland," Emma said, trying to stifle her own chuckle. "Our apologies. Now tell us, what do you do for the railroad and do you have any expectations for when it will arrive in Myers Ferry? I hope to see Patrick more often once it gets closer."

"Clyde, please, Mrs. Williams and ladies. I don't know what the joke is, but these mashed potatoes really are delicious."

"I made them," whispered the shy Mrs. Banks.

"Perhaps you will give me the recipe before I leave so I can pass it on to my wife," he said smoothly, but with a smile. "As to the railroad, we're getting closer to Myers Ferry every day and should be laying track through the town in another month or so. Then comes the hard part. The railroad plans to build a trestle to cross the river five miles upstream from here on terrain that allows for stable anchorage. I'm afraid there will be workers in and out of your town for a period of time once we arrive. The front office wants to headquarter in Myers Ferry while the trestle gets built. Once it's finished, of course we'll be moving on."

Married, Emma thought as the talk flowed on around her. *But that's all right. How nice it is being able to talk and laugh with a married man and not be labeled as no better than I should be.*

Apparently, the other women had similar thoughts because now there was no shortage of conversation, a couple of them showing a wide range of knowledge in national affairs Emma had not suspected.

Fade into the woodwork, indeed. Not in my house.

A good point to remember, she added to herself. Widows had more to talk about than just their children or grandchildren. Actually, most women did, married or not. She'd never realized how little she was expected to contribute to mixed conversation even when George was alive. He'd usually been the one to carry the conversational ball for them. Even at woman-centered occasions, the Ladies Aid meetings or the twice monthly quilting circle, for instance, conversation usually revolved around homelife or social gossip. Yet these same women read the newspaper as thoroughly as men did and certainly had their lives affected by the economic variables of the time.

But tonight, the two men and the several women were on equal footing, an event happening rarely at any time. Had the widows not contributed there would have been no conversation at all. Outnumbered, Clyde Suderland wouldn't stand a chance should he try to talk down to any of them.

Gentleman that he was, he didn't try and frankly seemed to enjoy himself, proving it as he left that night. "I enjoyed the evening and visiting with your friends, Mrs. Williams," he said as he shook her hand in farewell. "I hope I may visit again the next time Patrick comes home. Which should be more often now that the railroad is getting closer."

"Emma, please, Clyde. And you are always welcome. Come anytime."

The widows had seemed to enjoy the evening, too, but even so, at their next gathering Emma brought up the subject of Patrick's and Clyde Suderland's unexpected visit, asking the ladies if having men in attendance that evening had been uncomfortable for any of them.

The consensus was, not at all, though one of the women added that it helped that one of the males was related and the other not from Myers Ferry. Gossip, you know.

"As if we could be bothered with some woman's husband or one of the young bachelors in town," another huffed.

"I could be bothered," whispered Mrs. Banks.

֎

WITH THE RAIL construction drawing nearer to Myers Ferry every day, and Suderland tasked with laying the groundwork to set up the railroad's headquarters, Clyde and Patrick came more often, usually timing their visits for a Wednesday when the widows met at the Williams' home. Sometimes, Clyde came alone and, sometimes, brought along a friend or two. Sometimes those friends came alone or brought along a friend or two themselves. With the exception of Patrick, the men were always older. It didn't take Patrick long to figure out he could stay long enough to have a homecooked meal and then head out to join up with friends more his age.

Though the widows often gathered with just themselves in attendance, on those evenings when the gatherings were mixed certain agreements, spoken and unspoken, were upheld. For example, children, grandchildren and spouses, deceased or living, were never mentioned; nor, for that matter, was marital status. These mixed evenings of conversation or games or music were held for the sole purpose of relieving the boredom of loneliness, not as occasions for flirtation. No alcohol was served, and the evenings came to an end promptly at ten o'clock.

Emma made it quite clear to any visiting gentlemen that her house was not a bawdy house, merely a place for lonely people or those far from home to find some genteel company. If that was not what they were looking for, there were certainly other places in town more accommodating to their wants. Still, should a widow allow a gentleman to walk her home when the evening ended … well, that was no one's business but their own. The women were adamant that any untoward gossip originating from one of the attendees would find that person, widow or gentleman, no longer welcome.

As could be expected, word of the widows' exclusive little parties got around. Where before the town had ignored them individually, now, as a group, they'd become subjects of friendly interest. Yet with the exception of the Wednesday night gatherings, the widows went about their lives as they always had.

A few of the local men hinted at wanting to be invited but never were, the ladies determined there would be no gossip or inuendo where Myers Ferry husbands or bachelors were concerned. Widows, unless needing to be fed with a spoon, were still suspect when interacting with the town's men. That social isolation hadn't changed at all.

As for the women of the community, one of the wives at a Dorcas Literary meeting told Emma privately that as soon as her own husband died, she wanted to join. The widows seemed to have so much *fun,* she said. Emma told her that when the time came, she would be welcome.

A couple of marriages came out of the group over the

years. The shy Mrs. Banks became the shy Mrs. Whitoff and moved with her new husband further west. Even so, there were fewer marriages than one might expect. If a widow could manage for herself financially, most of them in the group preferred not to marry again, Emma included. Any liaisons of another sort were never mentioned.

Nor did Emma ever hint that on occasion, she slept exceptionally well, backed up against a nice warm wall of masculinity snoring in her ear.

ME AN' ANDY

We hold these truths
to be self-evident,
that all men and women
are created equal.

Elizabeth Cady Stanton (1848)

ME AN' ANDY

ME AN' ANDY GO BACK TO THE CRADLE – ANDY'S CRADLE, anyway.

Now I don't remember much about cradles, bein' just a tadpole myself, but once up an' movin', me an' Andy wore the same shadow. The Dawsons lived in the foreman's quarters alongside our Big House, so you might say us two young'uns had two homes and four parents.

Old Fort Davis was still goin' then, though things had quietened down a bit. Grierson and his buffalo soldiers had cleaned the Apaches out of West Texas, leavin' the ranchers without much to worry about but Mexican banditos, white desperados, and the occasional injun who didn't know he'd been licked. An' no rain.

Those were good years for youngsters growin' up in the Davis Mountains. Life was a lot slower when eighteen came in front of the date. For one thing, we didn't have radio to bring the world's meanness into the front parlor.

Me an' Andy took full advantage of the situation. Oh, we arggied and fought like all kids. Sometimes Andy'd have to eat dirt, sometimes me. But we never tattled on the other, an' when it came to snitchin' cookies from whichever ma's kitchen smelled the best, whoever did the snitchin' snitched two.

Andy never did catch up to me in inches, but grit and determination can't be measured by marks on a stick. Andy sure as heck wasn't gonna let me do anything by myself just because I was a few months older and a head or two taller.

Pa liked to tell the story of when he decided it was time for me to learn to ride. On a ranch, that's a big occasion for the oldest son. Ma came out to the corral to watch, an' so did the Dawsons. So did Andy.

All heck broke loose, Pa said, when Andy saw me sittin' tall on that ol' swaybacked horse. The hens didn't lay for a week. In the name of sanity there was nothin' to do but put Andy up behind me. Happy quiet descended an' the grownups grinned fit to kill, but it didn't last. Thirty seconds was about how long it took Andy to figger *behind* me could get permanent if allowed to continue. The upshot was, pretty soon we was ploddin' around the corral side by side, each on our own horse, with our daddies walkin' proud beside us.

Miz Dawson stopped laughin'. Ma stood beside her with an arm around her shoulders lookin' downright put out. That's when she looked at my pa and Mr. Dawson real level and said the words that put the seal on things.

"All right, you men," Ma said. "You've had your way today, settin' that baby up on a horse. It seems you've decided what one does, the other does as well. Well then, *so be it*," an' she and Miz Dawson walked back into the Big House, skirts blowin' in the wind, a war party of two withdrawin' just enough to find a better place for ambush.

Pa an' Mr. Dawson laughed. They laughed when Andy an' me got our first pair of high heeled boots. They laughed as they taught Andy an' me to use the lariat for ropin' more'n fence posts, an' were still chucklin' when they took Andy an' me on our first spring gather. Pa cackled like all get out when it turned out Andy was a better shot than me.

His smile didn't quite reach his eyes, though, when he walked into the Big House kitchen one afternoon an' found me washin' up the dishes from the noon meal. Ma, who'd been wipin' down the table, stood real quiet, watchin' him.

Pa didn't say anything for a minute, but then his laugh boomed out and he picked Ma up an' twirled her around, makin' her skirt bloom like a flower an' her cheeks grow rosy. "You warned me, I guess," he said, an' nuzzled her ear, makin' her hair fall down.

But that was the last laughin' Pa did for a while. He looked at me real cold and hard when he saw me crawl out from under the dinin' room table where I'd been polishin' the pedestal. An' his mouth got all straight an' grim one evenin' when Ma sat me down by the lamp an' had me sewin' buttons back on my shirts. "Don't you think you're takin' this a little far, Liz?"

Liz, not Lizzie like he usually called her.

Ma sat down on the other side of the little table that held the lamp and picked up one of Pa's shirts. She kept her eyes on her flyin' needle as she hemmed a cuff. "I could mend one of the saddles just as easy as you can if I had to," she said, an' her needle went real fast in an' out, in an' out of the cloth on the shirt's sleeve.

"That's different," Pa said.

"Is it?"

From where I sat I could see Ma's hands tremblin', but that needle kept flyin' in an' out, in an' out. Somethin' about the way she jabbed it in the cuff made me think she might be pretendin' it was Pa's hide.

Things came to a head one night when Pa came into supper just as I took a pan of biscuits out of the oven. I was proud of those biscuits – light as a feather and browned just right like Ma taught me.

When we was all seated at the table and Pa had given thanks an' filled his plate, I watched him pick up one of 'em, pride an' expectancy prob'ly written all over my face. My biscuit sat in his big work-hardened hand like a small cloud at sunset, an' when he broke it open, it came apart in two even halves just like it oughta. While they was still steamin' he slathered each side with butter so that it puddled into the biscuit like frostin' on warm gingerbread. He bit into it, chewed a minute, then swallowed. My eyes never left his face and his eyes never left mine.

He reached up an' used a finger to wipe a little butter off his mustache, his mouth tiltin' in the corners in the teeniest smile you ever saw. "Well, Clay," he said. "Looks like you're a dab hand at biscuit makin'. I don't think even your ma can make better."

Now that was high praise comin' from Pa, so why didn't I feel better about it? The only sound durin' the rest of the meal was knives an' forks hittin' the china.

When he finished eatin', Pa pushed his plate back a quarter inch with his thumb an' told the wall behind Ma's back, "Clay an' me are leavin' at first light in the mornin', Liz. The back range hasn't been checked in some time an' I want to know what stock I got back there. We'll be gone about a week."

Ma made a little movement but only said, "All right."

But I had to hold onto my chair I was so excited. "Really, Pa? You're gonna take us with you? Does Andy know?" an' I hopped up ready to hit the beaten path to the Dawson's house. The back range, full of canyons, dead ends, and deep draws was some of the meanest country in the Davis Mountains. That Pa was gonna take us with him was a *sign!*

"Hold it, Clay." I'd never heard Pa's voice so cold. Those biscuits turned to ice chunks down there in the bottom of my stomach. "This time it's just you an' me. Andy's not goin'. You're thirteen years old an' time you learned someday you'll be boss of this outfit an' not just the kitchen help," and he shot Ma a hard look before he scraped back his chair, grabbed his hat off the hook, an' headed out the back door without another word.

After the screen door slammed, I just sat an' looked at my greasy plate, tryin' to keep from bawlin'. Andy not goin'? Why, we always did ever'thing together. This trip was gonna be no fun atall.

Ma came out to see us off, standin' in the mornin' chill in her robe. I was already in the saddle, but Pa stood beside his horse.

"Lizzie," he said, fiddlin' with the reins, but Ma just stepped up an' hugged him.

"He'll be all right, you'll see," she said, but I don't know what Pa answered. Just then Andy came peltin' around the house, slid to a halt, then stood there, glarin'.

"Mornin', Andy," I called, polite-like, feelin' excited an' proud. Feelin' lonesome.

No answer. If looks could kill, I'd be a dead man today. A gray-eyed stare sizzled through the predawn gloom like a hot knife through lard. I sat lookin' straight ahead then, an' lonesome got mixed up with mad. Shoot, this wasn't my fault.

We had to ride our horses past Ma an' Andy to get out of the yard, an' at the last minute, out of corner of my eye, I saw Andy raise a hand. I raised a hand too an' grinned, but I don't think Andy grinned back. The spot between my shoulder blades tingled until we topped a rise an' dropped outta sight. By that time, I was glad to be goin'.

As we splashed through Limpia Creek with the rock palisades risin' up red an' tall on either side, an' the mornin' sun reachin' down to warm our backs, I began to feel pretty good. Andy was too durned little. I was with Pa all by myself because he thought I was big enough an' man enough to help clean out the back range. Right then I decided I'd die before I'd let Pa think he mighta been wrong.

It's a good thing I came to such a decision on that first mornin' because that was the last mornin' I found at all pleasant. Pa kept me in the saddle from can-see to can't. We beat the bushes for stock in ever' canyon an' draw in that godforsaken country, dodgin' catclaw an' horse cripplers one minute, windin' through thick stands of pine the next. The only time I got off a horse was when we were fixin' fence or I was on the roof of a line shack in the midday sun patchin' it. That night we slept inside, but mostly we camped under a jillion stars. As usual, we needed rain.

One night I was sittin' starin' in the fire as Pa prowled around seein' to supper. I held a cup of unmilked an' unsugared coffee in both hands because I was too plumb tuckered to hold it up with one. It was all I could do to keep my eyelids propped open enough not to disgrace myself.

"Biscuits," I mumbled, more to myself than to Pa.

"What?" he said.

"Biscuits," I repeated, an' yawned. "You brought me because of biscuits, not 'cause I'm bigger'n Andy."

Pa's face looked kinda funny there in the firelight an' he put the cover back on the Dutch oven. Then he chuckled. The sound rolled around and bounced off rocks till it came right back at us, an' for no reason I laughed, too.

"Well, I guess biscuits is what did it," Pa said when we'd stopped roarin' like jackasses. "But mainly I just wanted to find out what kinda man I'm raisin'."

That wiped the smile off my face in a hurry. Things got

real quiet an' I found I couldn't lift my gaze from the fire. I remembered all the cows hidden in the brush I'd rode right past, and the rope tosses I'd made an' missed. The cut on my hand started to throb where I'd been careless an' caught it on bobwire. Without thinkin', I fingered the rip in my pants leg, another bit of carelessness.

"Come get your supper, boy," Pa said.

When I'd filled my plate, I just kinda sat, wonderin' how I was gonna get any beans an' bacon past the lump in my throat.

"Found out you shoulda made these biscuits," Pa said around a mouthful.

I couldn't figger out how to duck my head any lower.

"Found out you're not a complainer." Pa forked another mouthful. "Found out you're not a quitter," an' he chewed some an' swallowed. "Found out you don't mind bein' showed how to do somethin'." He put his fork down an' looked at me straight. "Found out your ma an' me are pretty durn good parents 'cause we're raisin' a son to be proud of."

By this time, the lump in my throat was big as a boulder. "Th-thanks, Pa."

"No thanks to it, boy. Tomorra night you make the biscuits."

We stayed in the back range another two-three days. The mornin' we planned to leave, we got up to thunderheads buildin' all around us. "May be a wet ride home, Clay," Pa said, an' there was a wealth of satisfaction in the comment.

Well, sir, it was a little damp. If I hadn't been listenin' to the land slurpin' up the rain I'd've been miserable. Even with my slicker on, the wind blew water down my neck, then whipped around an' tossed it in my face. By the time we came to Limpia Creek I was so wet I squished, chilled to the bone, an' on the verge of feelin' mighty sorry for myself. But dry an' warm an' Ma were just a mile on the other side of the creek.

Wouldn't you know it'd be in flood. Pa looked at the creek an' looked at me. I knew what he was thinkin'. He wouldn't have hesitated if he'd been by himself.

"Pa, I can swim," I said.

"Swimmin' won't help much in that," he said, then seemed to make up his mind. He wanted to get home as bad as I did. "We'll ride down about a quarter of a mile where the water widens out some. Be past suppertime before we get home, but I reckon your ma won't mind."

So we headed the horses downstream, an' when we rode away from the roar of the creek to skirt a pile of boulders, Pa asked, "Where'd you learn to swim, boy?"

I puffed out my chest a bit. "Andy an' me taught ourselves down at the swirl two-three years ago," I said, tryin' to sound casual. The swirl was where a flood creek near the house was forced to take a sharp corner after hittin' a bluff of solid rock. Long after the creek was dry again, water remained pooled beneath the bluff. It was a good place to picnic or cool off on a hot summer's day.

"Just Andy an' you?" I heard surprise in Pa's voice.

When I said yes, he said kinda slow, "Swimmin' away from ever'one by yourselves like that isn't a real good idea, Clay. Anything could happen."

"Pa, that was a long time ago," I said, stung to think he thought I had such little sense. "Andy an' me was practic'ly babies then. We don't do stuff like that now."

Pa huffed a little like he was chokin' but then I realized he was laughin'. For the life of me I couldn't see the joke. We rounded the boulders back to where the creek broadened out and the water slowed some. It was time to cross the Limpia an' go home.

Somehow me an' Andy weren't together as much after

that. Pa kept me with him a lot, teachin' me what he thought I should know about runnin' the ranch. Ma still had me doin' chores around the house sometimes an' once when I complained to Pa, he told me real short that if I didn't want to mend my britches I should be more careful about rippin' 'em.

Andy was kept pretty busy too, an' we didn't have much playin' time anymore. Ever' once in a while we'd get a chance to ride out together an' talk things over like we used to, but not very often.

I guess because we weren't together much, it came as a real shock when Andy discovered skirts before I did.

Wait a minute. That don't sound right.

What I mean is, Andy found out how skirts could *flirt*. Heck, I was the oldest, even if it was only by a few months, an' it made me cockeyed mad.

Suddenly, seemed like ever' time I turned around, Jim Stiles an' Charley Fairfax were underfoot. So was Bobby White an' Jed Baxter. These town boys were sixteen an' seventeen years old an' Andy an' me were only fifteen then. Ever'body'd talk loud an' show off, an' I'd tell 'em how silly they was bein'. 'Course it didn't do the least bit of good, so I'd stomp off, leavin' Andy an' Jim an' Charley snickerin' behind me. Somehow, it was always me who felt silly.

Pa said I was a late bloomer an' not to worry about it, that it wouldn't be long before I joined 'em. Aloud, I said, 'yessir,' but privately I didn't think so. What was the big attraction, anyhow?

Andy'd get all gussied up an' next thing you knew, here'd come one or the other of those boys – or all of 'em – fillin' the Dawsons' front porch with the smell of foo-foo juice and mailorder hair oil. They'd be goin' to a dance at the school house in town, or to a party at one of the ranches, or a bunch of boys and girls would sit together gigglin' an' bein' coy at the church picnic. I never saw so much skirt swishin' in all my life.

Truth to tell, another year went by before I learned just how fascinatin' a swishin' skirt could be. One glimpse of Mary Helen Donahoe's big blue eyes and yellow curls could set me to sweatin' an' pantin' like I'd run a mile up the side of Livermore Mountain.

I never did cotton to the crowd Andy found so interestin' but I bought some foo-foo juice an' asked Bobby White the address of that hair oil outfit. There was a lot of us boys beatin' a trail to the Donahoe's white picket fence an' I needed all the help I could get. Next thing I knew, I'd joined the crowd at the church picnic an' did some laughin' myself, a few times with Mary Helen gigglin' beside me.

But we all get older an' some of the gigglin' stopped. I did a little hurrahin' more than I should an' Pa an' me came to words a time or two like boys an' their pas will. Mary Helen narrowed the field till only Kylie Moore an' me was still in the runnin'.

Andy an' me would prob'ly have gone our separate ways with no more'n childhood memories if I hadn't come home early one night from the Donahoes.

The moon was full an' bright an' shinin' like it only does in the Davis Mountains. I was hummin' to myself, feelin' real good, takin' the saddle off Brownie an' ready to turn him into the corral when I heard a funny little sound comin' from the dark side of the barn. Hangin' the saddle on the rail, I sorta cat-footed around it to see what was there.

Suddenly, I heard a curse to blister paint an' then all heck broke loose. It took a moment for me to figure out what all the flurry of cussin' an' thumps an' bumps was about. Neither of the two fighters knew I was there but when my eyes got used to the dark, I saw Jim Stiles half layin' on top of Andy with Andy's two arms pinned.

"Hell, Andy," he started to say. "I wasn't …."

That's all he said 'cause I took his shirt collar an' had him jerked off Andy faster'n you can spit. Andy's just a little thing, even full grown. Like dynamite with a lit fuse is little, maybe, but still not very big. All I could see through a red haze was Stiles' ugly face. I cocked an arm.

"You're outta line," Stiles said. "This is between Andy an' me. I wasn't gonna …."

I hit him. 'Course he hit me back an' then we were rollin' around on the dirt, punchin' an' gruntin' and goudgin' until an avalanche of water sloshed over our heads.

Andy set the bucket down, cool as you please. "I said I was all right. Jim, your horse is tied over at our porch. I suggest you fetch it an' go."

"An' don't come back," I added, still ready to beat him into the ground if he'd give me half a reason.

He didn't but stood there kinda quiet a minute as if waitin' for Andy to say somethin'. When the quiet got too loud for him, he looked at both of us real hard, then stomped around the side of the barn. We heard his footsteps as he made tracks for the Dawsons' house and his horse when he set his heels to it.

In the silence I didn't know what to say. This kinda thing had never happened before, with me fightin' Andy's fights. We walked around the barn to the corral an' I stuck my head in the horse trough, then used Andy's handkerchief to dry my face. While I was buried behind it, I asked, "You really all right?"

"Yes." Lookin' up at the moon shinin' back over my shoulder, Andy asked in a voice that sounded just as awkward as I felt. "How's Mary Helen?"

"Fine." I didn't want to talk about Mary Helen just then.

Shiftin' to the other foot, I folded the handkerchief just so and handed it back. "If you wash it in cold water, the blood'll come out," I said.

"You oughta know," Andy said, and laughed.

Durned if I didn't chuckle, too. Andy an' me had laughed a lot over my biscuit makin' and button sewin' an' it suddenly come to me that Andy was the only one I could laugh with over somethin' like that. With anyone else, even Mary Helen, I might've felt embarrassed. An' it come to me I'd missed that kinda laughter, the laughter of old times and shared summers, the laughter of someone laughin' with you an' not at you.

I watched Andy walk through the moonlight back to the Dawson's house and knew how close I'd come to lettin' a rare friendship drift right outta my life through neglect. I was gonna do somethin' about it.

I never had to.

A couple of days later, Pa came back to the Big House in the middle of the mornin' not feelin' good. Ma scolded an' clucked as she put him to bed, but you could tell she was scared. My pa was one of those people who is never sick, but he was sick then, with chills an' high fever, sometimes not knowin' who anybody was.

Ma an' me were kept busy full time tryin' to keep the hands fed, the ranch goin' an' one or the other of us with Pa twenty-four hours a day. The Dawsons were ever'where, doin' whatever had to be done, in the house or out of it.

An' when Pa passed on, which he did in just three short weeks, Mr. and Miz Dawson stood at the graveside either side of Ma, holdin' her up. Andy stood by me, holdin' my arm, and was still by me later that afternoon when I got out my horse an' rode hell for leather over the country with tears streamin' down my face till I couldn't cry no more. Then we stood together on a high mesa, not talkin', just watchin' the sunset. After a while, we walked the horses home. I was not quite twenty years old an' had a ranch to run.

For a couple of months, I stayed kinda numb, not havin' any time, really, to mourn. The spring gather had to be seen to, an' I was a brand-new boss tryin' to make sure I didn't let Pa's ranch go to hell in a handbasket. Mr. Dawson stayed on as foreman, though I called him Abe now like Pa done. He reminded me some of Pa, too, givin' me advice when I asked for it, then lettin' me take the consequences when I didn't follow it an' the back slappin' when I did. I was glad he was there. Sometimes I'd feel someone at my side an' Andy'd be there, too, only comin' to my shoulder maybe, but workin' hard enough for two men.

When the gather was over an' I had some of the cows shipped to market an' some of 'em moved to summer pasture, I finally had time to surface an' look around.

Came the day Andy an' me took the wagon into town. Ma needed some things, she said, but I guess mostly she thought I needed to get off the ranch. I admit to bein' glad to go. Spring had almost edged into summer an' the mountains stood sharp an' clear against a sky that was bluer'n a rancher usually likes to see. Andy an' me rode most of the way into town without sayin' a word, just enjoyin'.

The first person we saw was Mary Helen Donahoe. When we pulled up she was just walkin' out the door of the Mercantile, lookin' pretty as could be in a dress the same color as her eyes an' with her yellow curls spillin' out of her bonnet.

"Howdy, Mary Helen," I called.

She looked up at Andy an' me on the wagon seat an' her big blue eyes narrowed a bit. "Clay," she said, an' nodded a fraction to Andy.

"I see you been shoppin'," I said. Not the smartest

comment I coulda made but I suddenly felt the need of polite conversation.

I guess Mary Helen did, too. "Oh, you mean these," an' she nodded to her armload of parcels as if just rememberin' she held them. "Only a few things I needed to pick up for the wedding."

"Weddin'?"

Those big blue eyes widened to the size of saucers. "Why, Clay McDaniel. Don't tell me you didn't know me and Kylie are getting married the end of June."

Now, I'd be willin' to bet a month's wages she knew good an' well I didn't know no such of a thing, but she give me no time to say so. "I hope you and Andy will be able to come," she went on. "Goodness, look at the time. I must fly. So much to do, you know," an' she hurried down the street like a spotted dog was chasin' her, though I swear there was a smirk on her face.

I swung off the wagon, but Andy waited a minute, lookin' straight down into my face with those level gray eyes. "You all right?"

And you know? I was not only all right, I was relieved. So I looked back at Andy and I winked, but all I said was, "Her eyes're too big."

Andy laughed. In fact, we were both laughin' when we walked into the mercantile.

We was only about five miles outa town, headin' toward the ranch, when a feller with the biggest horse pistol you ever saw stepped out from behind some rocks.

"I got me a lame horse an' a lame partner," he said, real cool like. "I want your wagon." He was talkin' to me, but he was lookin' at Andy.

"No need to take the wagon, mister," I said. "Load your partner into the back an' we'll take him into town to the doc straight away."

The man didn't even look at me, just grinned and kept his eyes on Andy. "Mighty nice of you, boy, but I don't think my partner'd like that. Now get down or I'll shoot you down," and I knew he'd do it just as casual as he'd said it.

He had me. There was no way I could draw against a gun pointed right at my midsection. And if by some miracle he did miss, he'd prob'ly hit Andy. I got down an' Andy started to follow.

"Not you, little un," the man said. "We got a posse somewhere behind us lookin' for two men on horseback. I doubt they'd look twice at two men in a buckboard with a bitty mosquito like you along." He gave Andy a look that made my skin crawl.

Now I was really scared. There was no doubt in my mind this man intended to kill me – to be thinkin' of takin' Andy like that he'd have to – an' with me out of the way, Andy wouldn't stand a chance.

I must have made a sound because the next thing that horse pistol was lookin' at me with fixed intensity an' so was the man holdin' it. That was his first mistake.

"Mister," Andy said, and the rifle that had been behind the buckboard seat seconds ago didn't waver a hair, "It's time you dropped the gun."

The man laughed. "Because of a little button like you?" he sneered. "Not hardly." That was his second mistake and his last for a long time.

Andy shot him.

I've never seen such a surprised look on anyone's face. It prob'ly matched the look on mine. He grabbed his shoulder and stared at the blood gushin' into his hand like he couldn't believe his eyes. Then he turned up his toes and fainted into a heap on the road.

I knelt down to check him out an' get rid of his gun.

"Is he dead?" Andy was standing beside me with a face white as a wooly sheep.

"Nah, not even hurt bad." I stood up and tucked the feller's gun into my belt.

"Never could stand the sight of his own blood," a bitter voice said behind me. "Jimmy Jake spent a lifetime bein' all talk an' no sense."

I whirled around with my gun in my hand.

"But he's m'brother. What c'n I say?" The man, who looked weak an' sick, tossed a gun to my feet an' raised his hands skyward. "Be obliged if you'd take us into town," he said. "I'm tired of runnin'."

Jimmy Jake had come around by now, an' he moaned an' groaned an' complained all the way to the back of the wagon. But he kept a wary eye on Andy, which tickled me. I got the brothers settled, not even tyin' 'em. They both looked pretty awful an' I had all the weapons.

When I came back around the wagon, I found Andy leanin' up against the front wheel, shakin'. I wasn't sure what to do so I just kinda reached out. Next thing I knew, Andy had both arms around my waist, cryin' into my shoulder.

Well, I can tell you, I've never been so shocked in all my life. I didn't know what to do with my hands or what look to wear on my face.

Andy mumbled into my shirt.

"What?" I croaked. By this time, I could hardly talk.

"I missed," Andy said, and pulled back a little. It was prob'ly a good thing those gray eyes was wet because the sparks in 'em woulda set a grass fire. We needed rain. "I thought that rascally so'n'so was going to kill you and I was aiming at his heart. It's the first time since I was ten years old I've missed what I was shooting at." The tears was really comin' now. "If he hadn't been such a b-baby about his own blood you'd be d-dead by now and I just wouldn't be able to *stand* it."

Well, heck. When somebody's weepin' over the thought of you dyin' an' you're feelin' kinda shaky over the thought your own self, an' a sweet little mouth is that close to yours – well, a feller'd be a fool not to kiss it. So I did. It felt mighty good, too, so I did it again, standin' there in the middle of the road under that big West Texas sky.

I'd prob'ly have gone on kissin' Andy some little while if Jimmy Jake hadn't said in a nasty voice, "Could we get this show on the road? I don't feel s'good an' you two ain't helpin' any."

I jerked back like a scalded cat an' I know my face was red as a New England barn, but Andy just said in a voice that'd bend nails, "Jimmy Jake, perhaps I should see if my aim's improved in the last five minutes."

That shut him up, but the moment, as they say, was lost. Andy an' me climbed into the wagon an' I turned the team around to head back to Fort Davis. Andy sat close enough for an arm an' shoulder to rub up against mine an' the feel of 'em did interestin' things to my equilibrium.

"We make a good team, Andy," I said after a while, an' cleared my throat. "Reckon we oughta make it permanent?"

Andy chuckled, tucked a hand through my arm, an' kissed me on the cheek. "I've been planning on it since I was twelve," she said.

Jimmy Jake growled kinda digusted-like, but Andy an' me just laughed.

Y'know, I thought Andy's folks an' my ma would be shocked, but they wasn't the least bit surprised.

Andy an' me have been together now for over forty years, standin' shoulder to shoulder through wet times an' dry, fat times an' lean. We lost a boy in the Great War who'd been mad about airplanes. Andy still takes flowers to the place we set aside for him in the family cemetery. But it's just a space. He's buried somewhere in Europe.

Our daughter an' her husband run the ranch now, an' we're all hopin' our two grandsons won't follow the uncle they never knew to Germany. That feller Hitler is makin' some pretty strange noises.

Please God, the next places on the hill will belong to us old folks. We're ready. Prob'ly the kids will want to carve CLAYTON MICHAEL MCDANIEL and ANDREA MARIE DAWSON MCDANIEL on the stones, but I told 'em it'd be a sight cheaper an' a whole lot truer if they'd just use one stone an' carve on it, ANDY AN' ME.

ABOUT THE AUTHOR

Long ago, d. j. Rangel earned an Interdisciplinary B.A. degree with a major in history and a minor in literature. As kind of an afterthought but with the idea of actually earning a living with such a degree, she tacked on education certification. Which turned out to be a good move since over the years she wound up teaching everything from pre-K to community college and adult ed. In between those two extremes, her teaching experience involved trying to get middle school students to take an interest in Texas history, and teaching a summer course in U.S. post-Civil War history to high school students who needed it to graduate.

d.j. has also traveled extensively, including two stints with the Peace Corps, one to the Republic of the Philippines, the other more recently to the Republic of Armenia, stints focusing on working in the schools of these respective countries. The history of both these republics, past and present, is fascinating. Still, d.j.'s pole star remains pointed to the U.S. West, specifically the Southwest, though *The West* in general exerts a pull like no other. As a seasonal park ranger with the National Park Service, she served at Fort Davis National Historic Site in Far West Texas and at Bent's Old Fort National Historic Site in Southeastern Colorado, both with living history programs. If *those* don't stir up the imagination juices, nothing will, so don't forget that minor in literature that was never formally used inside a classroom.

d.j. is, and always will be, a prolific reader of both fact and fiction, contemporary and historical. Now, finally, she gets to write and indulge her U.S. Western history fixation in creating short stories, some based on true accounts, some purely imaginary.

Made in the USA
Columbia, SC
27 June 2020